I0618427

MIRRORED

By Dalia Florea

Published by Dalia Florea at CreateSpace

ISBN-13: 978-0615937441

ISBN-10: 0615937446

© 2013, 2017 by Dalia Florea

ALL RIGHTS RESERVED. This book contains material protected under International and Federal Copyright Laws and Treaties. Any unauthorized reprint or use of this material is prohibited. No part of this book may be reproduced or transmitted in any form or by any means, electronic or mechanical, including photocopying, recording, or by any information storage and retrieval system without express written permission from the author.

All characters in this book are fictional and have no relation to anyone bearing the same name or names. They are not even distantly inspired by any individual known or unknown to the author, and all incidents are pure invention.

For questions about this book contact Dalia Florea

www.daliafloreabooks.com

Cover design by Cover Me Book Covers

AUTHOR'S MESSAGE

When I first wrote MIRRORED, I didn't know much about writing a novel, and I believe I offered it to the world before it was ready.

Now it's ready. If you read the first version and are now reading this one, thank you! I hope I am offering a much better story to you. If you are reading this for the first time—ignore me and enjoy the story.

CHAPTER 1

Springtime in New York City didn't offer as many of the beautiful flowering blooms of azalea shrubs and the pink and white blossoms of dogwood trees as I experienced growing up in Charlotte, North Carolina. But I could still feel springtime in the air as I walked briskly down the sidewalks of lower Manhattan, looking like a working-class Paula Patton channeling Audrey Hepburn in a black and white striped blouse, black pencil skirt, and red heels. The air wasn't all that fresh above ground, but it sure beat the smell of urine in the subway station.

I stopped at Midtown Bagels to grab my usual breakfast. And, as I reached the front of the line, Luiz, a short stubby-looking, olive-skinned man, tapped in the amount I owed on the cash register.

"Nicole Watkins. Just like you like it," he said with a big grin on his face, handing me a bag containing my breakfast. "A bagel with cream cheese, and a coffee with cream and two sugars."

He got it just right, too. *I should trip him up one day and order something different.* I did love that he knew exactly what I liked and had it ready every morning when I came into the cafe.

"How many times do I have to tell you to call me Nikki?"

"Your credit card says Nicole Watkins."

I shook my head and laughed. Ever since the first day I came in here, when I paid for my first bagel, he looked down at my debit card, read my name and had been calling me by my full name ever since.

"How are you today, Luiz?" I asked.

"You're looking at it," he said as another customer approached, interrupting him before he got a chance to say more. I didn't know what he meant by that but I smiled anyway. When I looked back to wave, his attention had already shifted to helping other customers that flowed into the shop.

New York City was unlike any city that I'd ever lived in. Tall buildings invading the sky, cars jammed in traffic with drivers laying on their horns, the smell of food coming from street vendors, street hustlers trying to lure pedestrians to either play card games or to buy their wares, and crowded sidewalks where everyone seemed to be in a hurry to get somewhere or another.

I was in a hurry, too, still trying to distance

myself from my divorce from Michael after three long years.

******

As I sat at my desk going through my notes and preparing to go to the 23rd precinct in Harlem to interview Detective Andre Moore, my boss poked his head inside my cubicle.

"Ms. Watkins, this is your first field assignment," Mr. Blackman said, seeming to read my facial expression.

Ryan Blackman was an Irish man in his late sixties, stocky, with silver hair and a thick mustache, bright blue eyes, and a kind smile. He could be tough, but he also had a gentle side. He was shrewdly intelligent, and I figured I could learn a lot from him. He had taken over the newspaper, *News Today* when his father died of lung cancer seven years ago. He had extensive experience as a field reporter, but running a newspaper meant he had to take on new skills. Since Mr. Blackman had worked alongside his father before he became ill, he had gotten to know a little something about running a newspaper.

"I want to make sure you're prepared for this interview–"

"I'm ready." I apparently interrupted his spiel because the look he gave me was one of reprimand with a twist of 'don't try my patience'. I recoiled a little.

He continued, "...Especially with the nature of the case. I need to know you can handle the details—"

"Absolutely Mr. Blackman. I can handle it." But once again, I had interrupted him and the grimace on his face let me know that I needed to put my enthusiasm in check.

Blackman continued as if he hadn't heard my reassurances. "I can't afford any fuck ups."

I shook my head to reassure him there'd be no fuck ups. I opened my mouth to say as much then caught myself before a single syllable spilled off my tongue.

"I want to be the first to run this story," Blackman said sternly. "And I need everything you can dig up on this one."

There was a long pause. I sat quietly for a few beats not sure if it was safe to insert my reassurances and enthusiasm. But the silence wore me down. As I opened my mouth to fill the silence, he reached out and put his hand on my shoulder as a father does a child.

"I had to pull a lot of strings to get you this interview. *Don't* make me regret it."

As Blackman turned to leave my cubicle, my mind drifted to the rumors circulating around office about the newspaper being in bad financial shape. If the paper didn't get any financial backing, it would go bankrupt. The weight and worry of the paper's solvency showed in the lines of Blackman's face. Although I had hoped it was just a rumor, I wasn't worried about it too much. My plans didn't include staying at the paper for long. It had been the only place that would hire me with no journalism experience. Besides that, my ultimate goal was to own and publish a fashion magazine. I returned my focus to the notes I'd taken suddenly realizing how much this interview could mean for this newspaper's survival.

"Ms. Watkins," Blackman said, peering over the top of the cubicle. He had startled me. I thought he'd walked away. As my wide-eyed gaze met with his, he said, "This story has a deadline, so don't waste valuable time."

He stood silent for a moment looking me in the eyes as if he were assessing me – sizing me up, then said, "I want your write-up on my desk by the close of business today." If he was trying to impress upon me the fast-paced nature of the business, he had succeeded. And, before I could respond, he disappeared down the long row of cubicles.

I was nowhere near as confident as I led Mr. Blackman to believe – if he even believed me at all.

I think I was trying to convince *myself* more than I was trying to convince *him* that I was ready. The pressure was on, and now I had to pull a rabbit out of my hat by end of business. If I hadn't broken out in a cold sweat yet, it was because my mother used to say, "God doesn't give us more than we can handle, baby." I was praying that this was one of those situations. I swallowed hard, still wondering if I was taking on more than I could handle.

I was assigned a story on a brutal rape-homicide that had occurred in Harlem. Someone had brutally raped and then stabbed a sixteen-year-old girl twenty-two times in the apartment complex where she lived with her single mom and two younger brothers. I decided to skip lunch, afraid I wouldn't be able to keep any food down when I read the gruesome details. Just the thought of what had happened to that young girl made me nauseous. Growing up in an upper middle-class neighborhood in Charlotte, North Carolina, I hadn't had any experience with violent crimes like this. In fact, I couldn't remember even seeing a policeman come into the neighborhood. I had lived in an area where our neighbors were lawyers, doctors, and bankers.

My father was a cardiologist and my mother was a stay-at-home mom. Mom had attended college and had gone on to get her master's in education. She taught elementary school for a few years until she became pregnant with me. When I was three, my mom became pregnant again. I later learned that her pregnancy had been normal and healthy until a few weeks before her due date. When she didn't feel the normal movements of the baby one day, she became concerned, and my father rushed her to the hospital. The emergency room doctor did an ultrasound to check for the baby's heartbeat—and there was none. The baby had died. I was much too young to remember anything during that time but could imagine the heartache my parents had endured. My mother never tried to have another child after that experience. I guess it was just too painful.

I grabbed my purse and briefcase and headed to the elevator. While waiting for the elevator, I took a quick look in the mirrored wall adjacent to the elevator doors and noticed a button had come undone on my blouse. *Better fix this—don't want Detective Moore getting any bright ideas.* I fastened the offending button.

The doors to the elevator opened and I stepped inside, pressing the button to the lobby. As the door proceeded to close, Stanley Pittman stuck his hand in, preventing the door from shutting. *Good grief.* I avoided eye contact as I was not up for a conversation with this egotistical, chauvinistic jerk. Unfortunately, my tactic didn't work.

"Well ... hello, Ms. Watkins," he said, emphasis on "Ms."

I shot him a look of annoyance but didn't utter a word.

Judging from the smirk on his face, he seemed to enjoy the fact that his presence annoyed me. *Damn it! Why do I let this piece of slime get under my skin?* Although physically he looked like a male model right off the pages of a magazine—tall, tan, toned, sandy blonde hair, brown eyes, and a bright smile full of beautiful white teeth—his personality and demeanor were nothing short of ugly. I think the man actually loathed women, taking every opportunity to belittle and sabotage them in some way. I felt sorry for the fools who got caught up in his looks and his false sense of charm.

Stanley Pittman had come to work at the newspaper about a year ago as a photojournalist. Considering his arrogance, I thought he would have been more comfortable in front of a camera than behind one.

"So ...where are you headed?" he asked, a plastic grin on his face.

As the door to the elevator opened, I turned to him and said, "I don't see why that would be any of your business." I exited the elevator and pushed through the revolving doors that led out of the building.

Still rush hour, people filled the sidewalks, cars still jammed the streets, and drivers still honked their horns.

I headed down the subway stairs to catch the Lexington Avenue line uptown to East Harlem, better known as Spanish Harlem and El Barrio. Surprisingly, I found an empty seat on the train. I pulled out my compact mirror to freshen my makeup, dabbing a little translucent powder on my nose and forehead to take the shine away. Retrieving my notes from my briefcase, I scanned them quickly to be sure I'd captured all the pertinent information about the case.

I'd never been inside a police station before, but I could say that the building was much larger than the Charlotte police stations I'd seen on the news. As I reached the door, scenes from the television show *Law and Order* flashed through my mind. I entered the building and saw a male police officer in uniform sitting at the front desk. There were desks in the area behind him—some empty and others occupied with people doing what looked like clerical work — typing or on the telephone. No police detectives gathered at a desk discussing a case with their captain like on TV. *No*, I decided. It was nothing like *Law and Order*.

Detective Moore had instructed me to inform the desk sergeant that he was expecting my visit. I was about to approach the man at the desk in front of me, assuming he was the desk sergeant, when a uniformed police officer walked up and said, "Sarg, we have a problem—one of the perps in the cell claims he's sick." The officer at the desk noticed my presence and lifted one finger to the other police officer, indicating he would be with him in a moment.

"Can I help you, miss?"

"Uh … yes … I'm Nicole Watkins. I'm a reporter with *News Today*. I'm here to see Detective Andre Moore. He's expecting me."

He looked at me expectantly, "I need to see some ID."

"Oh, of course," I said as I dug into my purse to get my associated press identification card.

He looked at it and held it as he picked up the telephone receiver and dialed a number. "Moore? Davidson here. You have a visitor. A Ms. Nicole Watkins from the newspaper." He doodled on a sheet of paper on the desk as he waited for a reply from the detective. "Yeah, I see. Okay … I'll send her up." He hung up and gave me back my ID card. He pointed to a door that led to a stairway. "Go through that door and up the stairs to PDU ..."

He must've seen the puzzled look on my face.

"I'm sorry, Police Detective Unit. That's the Detective Bureau. Detective Moore's office is two doors down on the right when you come out of the stairway."

I thanked him and proceeded in the direction of the stairs. Exiting the stairwell, I stood in a long hallway with several offices. My footsteps echoed on the uncarpeted floor with each step I took. The décor looked a little dated. The doors to the offices were labeled with the detectives' names. As I reached the second office from the stairway, I saw that the door stood open.

The name on the door read Detective Andre Moore. A man stood inside, his back to me. I was sure he'd heard me clacking down the hall, but he was deeply engrossed in his phone conversation and didn't turn around. From behind, he looked about 6-4. He wore black slacks and a burgundy polo shirt, and I could see that his body was in great shape—athletic and toned. I couldn't help myself from zeroing in on his firm butt.

He moved around to the other side of his desk and turned to face me, and I found myself suddenly breathless. He was the most beautiful man that I'd ever laid eyes on. I know that men aren't usually described as beautiful, but he was definitely more than handsome. Thick, shiny dark hair, yellowish-brown skin, hazel eyes ... and those lips! I could almost taste them. His eyes met mine, and I felt my heart race.

He motioned for me to come in and have a seat.

I stood paralyzed for a few seconds. I remember reading about this kind of attraction in romance novels but never believed the hype. I pulled myself together, hoping that he hadn't noticed my flushed face, and sat down in one of the chairs in front of his desk.

He hung up the telephone, stood, and reached over to shake my hand. "As you might have already guessed, I'm Detective Andre Moore, but please, call me Andre."

I blushed as I lifted my hand to touch his. For a moment, words got stuck in my mouth. I cleared my throat. "I'm Nicole Watkins. Nice to meet you." I reluctantly released his hand.

"Can I get you something to drink, Ms. Watkins? Water? Soda?"

My nerves seemed to be taking over. *I've got to put this schoolgirl silliness to the side and do the job I'm here to do.* "No, thank you. I'm ready to discuss the case.

Oh, and please call me Nicole." *Darn, why did that slip out?*

Detective Moore had the case file on his desk and I grabbed my notebook and a pen from my briefcase so that I could take notes as well as review the questions I needed to ask about the case. I looked up to find him watching me. I couldn't quite read his expression—he gave nothing away— and his eyes returned to the file on his desk. There was something about the way he looked at me that stirred my soul.

"Are you ready for this," he asked.

I shrugged. "I guess I'm as ready as I'll ever be."

He proceeded to describe the case from its beginning, going over the reports of the officers who had first arrived at the murder scene.

Detective Moore said, "Mrs. Rojas had discovered the body of her sixteen-year-old daughter, Vanessa, lying in a pool of blood in one of the bedrooms of the apartment, her body covered with stab wounds and bruises." He removed a couple of pictures from the folder and handed them to me. "Here, take a look at these. This is what that monster did to this poor girl."

I took the pictures, feeling hesitant and uneasy. Taking a deep breath, I tried to mentally prepare myself, but nothing could have prepared me for what I saw. There in the pictures, a young girl lay with bruises, blood, and multiple cuts all over her small, naked, lifeless body. The bedcovers were stained with blood. I couldn't bear to look anymore and handed the pictures back to him.

"What kind of person does that to another human being, much less a child?" My voice sounded strangled. Dizziness enveloped me as I visualized that brutal scene in my head. I hoped it wasn't noticeable.

Before I could recover, Andre pushed away from his desk and rushed over to me. Kneeling beside me and placing his hand on my forearm, he asked, "Are you okay? Can I get you some water? I apologize—I should have warned you about what was in those pictures. We don't have to continue." He seemed to have a look of genuine concern in his eyes.

I inhaled deeply, trying to gulp as much air as possible. "I'll be fine, I just need a minute," I said, regaining my composure.

"Ms. Watkins ... um ... Nicole, we don't have to do this now ... I—"

Remembering Blackman's warning that he had pulled a lot of strings to get this interview, I decided that now was not the time for me to get emotional. I had to suck it up and get this done.

"Detective, I'm fine. Really I am. Let's continue."

Still kneeling next to me, looking into my eyes, he asked, "Are you *sure* you're okay? Even veteran police officers have a hard time dealing with crimes as horrific as this one."

I shifted in my chair. "I'm fine. Let's do this. I've got a deadline to meet."

He stood and moved back behind his desk. He tucked the pictures back into the folder and glanced up at me.

"Go on, Detective."

He raised his eyebrows. "Not comfortable calling me Andre?"

I glanced away for a second, not sure how to answer his question because on some level I did feel uncomfortable calling him Andre—but I didn't know why. "Well, if it's going to help speed this along, Andre it is."

I don't know why I was being so defensive toward this man who had been nothing but a gentleman toward me since I arrived in his office. Maybe I was feeling a little vulnerable because he had witnessed my emotional reaction to those ghastly photos. I just couldn't imagine coming home and finding my daughter ... It suddenly struck me to ask who had called the police.

"How were the police notified? I mean ... who made the call?"

Detective Moore shuffled through the pages of the report. "Some neighbors heard the screams and called nine-one-one, but before the police arrived, her mother had come home from work. Apparently, the victim was supposed to have picked up her younger brothers from school but never showed up. The school had called the mother to let her know."

My stomach felt queasy. "What an awful thing for a mother to stumble upon, poor woman." I looked at Detective Moore as another horrible thought crossed my mind. "What about the children? Vanessa's two younger brothers. Were they there when the mother went into the apartment?" I was almost afraid to hear the answer.

He looked up at me, and the sadness in his voice matched the look in his eyes. "No, the little boys were with a neighbor," he said, seeming to maintain a stoic expression. "The mother stated that when she arrived at the apartment, the door was unlocked, which wasn't normal. She said she had a bad feeling about it and thought that it best to let the boys wait at a neighbor's apartment while she went in to check on her place. She thought she might have been robbed because her place had already been broken into twice in the past year."

Why such sadness from a homicide detective

who had probably worked a zillion homicide cases? "Detective ... uh ... Andre, may I ask a question?"

He looked at me expectantly. "Sure, isn't that why you're here? To ask questions?"

I smiled. "I guess I deserved that."

Smiling back at me, he asked, "What is it? What do you want to know?"

Rolling my pen between my fingers, I asked, "How long have you been a homicide detective?"

He leaned back in his chair, seeming to give some thought to the question. "I've been working on homicide cases for about ten years now. I've seen it all, but this case is different." He seemed to wander off in thought for a minute. "Why do you ask?"

I crossed one of my legs over the other and studied him for a moment. "Surely you've seen cases similar to this. What makes this one so special? Is it the victim's age?"

He opened one of the drawers to his desk and appeared to be taking something out but changed his mind and shut the drawer again. "You're probably right. I guess that's what makes it different."

I silently wondered what he'd been about to take out of that drawer and I had the feeling that it was more than the age of the victim that disturbed him. Did he know this family personally? No, that couldn't be it. He had seemed detached when discussing the case until I had asked the question about the children. Snapping out of my reverie, I continued to ask a few more questions from my notes, and he offered more details, all of which would be really helpful for my story.

"Andre, would you mind describing the neighborhood where this took place? I'm fairly new to New York, and I'm still learning about the various neighborhoods. I'd like some specifics on the scene of the crime for my article."

He grinned. "So where are you from? How long have you lived in New York?"

Why do I get the impression that he's fishing for information about my personal life? Well, I suppose it's my own fault—I kind of set myself up. Then again, maybe a part of me wants him to know. "I'm from Charlotte, North Carolina. I moved to New York about three years ago after ... uhhh ... never mind."

He raised an eyebrow. "After what? You were about to say more."

I was not about to discuss my divorce with Detective Moore. "And I also said never mind. It's nothing. Now would you mind giving me some information about the neighborhood?"

He stared at me for a moment with those

beautiful hazel eyes and I felt my body warming. "I can do better than that."

Had his voice deepened when he said those words or was it my imagination? I found myself hypnotized by his eyes—I swear I could see his lips moving but I wasn't hearing a single word that came out. Then I came to my senses.

"Uhh ... huh?"

He grinned. "You seemed pretty spaced out for a minute there. You okay?"

My face felt flushed. "Yes, I'm fine."

He picked up his phone and started dialing. As he did so, he said, "I'm going to get clearance for you to ride with me over to the Lincoln Houses. This way you can actually see where the victim lived."

I nodded in appreciation and gathered my things while he was on the phone.

He finished his phone call and looked up. "Just give me a minute to clear my desk, then we can head out. Would you like to stop to get something to eat on the way? I haven't eaten lunch yet, and judging from the time you arrived in my office, you haven't either." He stood and grabbed some keys from his desk drawer.

I stood as well. "I'm not sure I have time for a break. I have to get back to the office as soon as we leave the Lincoln Houses. This story has to be on my boss' desk before I leave work tonight."

As we exited his office, he closed the door behind us. Neither of us spoke. The only sound was the clicking of my heels against the hard, shiny floor. It was definitely an uncomfortable silence. We walked past the stairway I had used earlier and down the hall to a door leading to another stairway. Taking the stairs down, we arrived at a door that exited into a lot where several cars were parked, including two police patrol cars.

Detective Moore waved to a uniformed officer standing near one of the cars. The police officer waved back.

I kept pace with him until he stopped at one of the unmarked cars. The silence between us was killing me. I guess I could have struck up a conversation, but I couldn't think of anything to say. Was he upset that I had turned down his offer for lunch? He came around to the passenger side of the car and held the door open for me.

"Thank you," I said as I slid into the front seat of the car.

When he got into the driver's seat and turned the key in the ignition, he looked over at me. "I absolutely have to stop for something to eat. How about if we grab something on the way and eat in the car?"

I had to admit I was hungry, but I didn't want to waste any time because I had to get back to the office. I also had to factor in the amount of time it would take to travel by subway.

He must have read my mind because he interrupted my thoughts. "I'll drive you back to your office, Nicole."

I looked at him, biting my lip. "I wouldn't want you to go out of your way."

He glanced at me before steering the car out of the lot. "Not a problem. It would be my pleasure. So, what would you like to eat?"

"A salad will be fine," I replied.

"A salad?"

"Yes."

"A salad. Really? You trying to watch your weight?"

Do I tell him that I really *like salad?* "Well ..."

"You don't need to," Andre said. "I think you look just fine to me."

I blushed. "Thank you."

Do I return the compliment? I hardly know the man.

But I do believe I want to know him more ...

CHAPTER 2

I had finished my last bite of lettuce when we approached a housing project. The buildings were all tall. They seemed to be more than thirteen floors high.

Detective Moore, or *Andre* as he prefers, cut the engine. "Are you ready?"

I wasn't sure if I was. I had never done a story on this level and didn't know what to expect. Although there was a little adrenaline running through my veins, my stomach was turning flips. Maybe it wasn't such a good idea to eat first.

"When you said that you were going to show me the building, I didn't expect that we would be going up to the apartment."

As he turned toward me, his hazel eyes sparkled against the rays of the sun shining into the car. "Nicole, if you want your story to be interesting and if you want to be better than the other reporters, here's your chance for an exclusive with the girl's mother."

"What if she doesn't let us in?"

"I'll convince her that I'm here to do a follow-up."

"Yeah, but ..."

Andre unleashed his seatbelt, got out of the car, and came around and pulled my door. I glanced at my watch before stepping out, calculating how much time it would take for me to wrap this up and get back to work. Blackman wouldn't mind what time I came back, as long as I had a good story.

"What if..."

"Don't worry. You'll be fine." He offered his hand.

We waited for traffic to clear before jaywalking to the other side of the street. A group of young men congregated close to the entrance of the building as we neared. They didn't seem to notice us as we entered the building.

The building smelled of cigarettes and urine. Andre pressed the button to the ninth floor once we were inside the elevator. My stomach began to turn flips again.

"Are you okay?" Andre asked.

"I'm fine."

The door slid open to the ninth floor. There was

an apartment door facing the elevator when we stepped off. Apartment Nine-A. Andre turned left and walked along the dimly lit corridor with me trailing him. He stopped in front of apartment nine-G. He glanced at me before lifting the door knocker. I gave him a nervous smile then slid my sweaty palm down the side of my skirt. The few seconds that passed before the door opened seemed like minutes.

A petite Latino woman, who appeared to be in her forties with long dark curly hair hanging at her shoulders, pulled open the door. Her eyebrow furrowed and her lips pressed together.

"Are you Ms. Rojas?" Andre asked.

"*Sí*, yes."

"I'm Detective Andre Moore and this"—he pointed at me—"is Ms.Watkins, a reporter with *News Today*."

She stared at me and absently brushed her hair back with her hand. "No one told me that the police was coming back or a reporter. Are you from the TV station?"

"No ma'am," I said. "I'm with the newspaper."

"Ms. Rojas, may we come in to ask you a few questions?" Andre asked.

"I've already told the police what I know. What else is there to tell?"

"Maybe our questions will help you to remember

something that you might not have been able to remember before," I said.

Her friendly brown eyes were puffy and swollen. She nodded and opened the door further to let us in. She fastened her blue sweater around her as she led us past a kitchen into what appeared to be a living room. The room was small and cozy. Photos of a young girl's journey from infancy to her teenage years covered the wall. A metal stand with a few live plants on it sat in front of the window. The aroma of fiery spices seeped through from the kitchen.

"Please sit." Ms. Rojas pointed to a gold couch pressed against the wall near the window. "Can I offer you something to drink?"

"No, thank you," Andre said.

I shook my head. My eyes caught what appeared to be a school photo of Vanessa smiling, a stark contrast to what Andre had shown me at the station.

"What is it you want to know?" Ms. Rojas asked as she looked from Andre to me.

Andre gestured to me as if he wanted me to start asking the questions.

"Would you mind if I take out my recorder? It's to help me remember, and it's easier than writing notes." I dug into my leather bag for the recorder.

"Go ahead," Ms. Rojas said.

I placed the recorder on the glass-topped coffee

table and pressed the record button. "Can you tell ... us ... what your daughter was like?"

I glanced at Andre, who had pushed back onto the sofa.

"Well, what do you mean?" she asked.

"What was her personality like? Was she a good student?"

"My Vanessa. She is ... was a good girl. She helped me take care of her two younger brothers." Tears filled her eyes. "You know, she wanted to be a doctor for animals. She was gonna go to college."

"Ms. Rojas, this must be very painful for you to talk about, but your story will help others and hopefully the police catch the person who did this." My eyes moved to Andre for assurance.

He glanced at me but didn't say anything.

"The day that you found Vanessa, were you alone?" I asked.

A tear rolled down her cheek as she stared at the floor. Her hand gripped the tissue she had pulled from the box on the table. She nodded.

"Can you take us to that day and tell us what you saw?"

She unraveled the tissue and blew her nose into it. "Give me a minute." She choked back tears.

I pushed the recorder across the table closer to her while she pulled herself together.

She cleared her throat. "Vanessa usually picks the boys up from school because I get off work too late to pick them up. That day, I got a call from my boys' school because they hadn't been picked up. I called Vanessa right away to find out where she was. Oh God!" She clutched her sweater at her chest. I pulled a fresh Kleenex and handed it to her.

"Thank you," Ms. Rojas said. "I couldn't reach her. I had to leave work to pick up the boys. When I got here, it was odd that the door was unlocked. I had a funny feeling come over me. Something wasn't right. Something told me not to bring the boys in here with me. I took them next door to my neighbor, Ms. Brown."

I glanced at Andre, who seemed to be listening intently. My focus returned to Ms. Rojas.

"I didn't notice anything out of place or unusual at first," Ms. Rojas said. "I peeked in the boys' room and saw the normal mess they kept. At the door to Vanessa's room ... oh my ..." She started shaking. "I can't. I'm sorry but I can't." She sobbed.

"It's okay, Ms. Rojas," I said. "You don't have to say anymore. Would it be okay if I take a look in Vanessa's room?"

She wiped her eyes, nodded, and stood. We followed her down the short hall. She pointed towards Vanessa's room then disappeared back down the hall.

Andre stepped aside and allowed me to enter first.

Aligned next to the purple pillows on Vanessa's bed were three ragdolls. Purple seemed to be her favorite color. Purple curtains, purple lampshades, purple throw rug—and a purple beanie bag sat in the corner of the room. I walked over to the wooden white dresser to take a closer look at some of the things on it. Shea butter lotion, a bottle of Guess Girl perfume, a clear plastic organizer filled with hair accessories, and in the far-right corner was a purple music box. I ran my fingers across it.

"Nicole?"

I turned to face Andre.

"I'm going to go check on Ms. Rojas," he said.

I nodded.

I lifted the bottle of perfume and sniffed it. It had a fruity sweet smell. I closed my eyes letting the aroma stay with me. I returned to the music box and opened it. A ballerina dressed in a purple tutu twirled to "Swan Lake." As the music played, I crossed the small bedroom and sat on the edge of the bed and peered out the window. *When she looked out of this window the morning of the day she was murdered, what did she see? Did she see hope? Did she see a shining future?* My eyes filled with tears as a memory flashed of her stiff body lying in a pool of blood on *this* bed.

I jumped to my feet and hurried out of the room. I needed to get out. I needed air. This was all too much.

Ms. Rojas seemed to be in a calmer state as she sat across from Andre. I gathered my things. "Thank you for your time, Ms. Rojas."

Andre stood. "Nicole, are you okay?"

"Can we go, please?" I didn't wait for a response and moved toward the door. I heard him thanking Ms. Rojas as I exited the apartment.

He caught up with me at the elevator. "What happened?"

I stared down at the dull tiled floor. "It got to be too much, that's all."

The elevator door slid opened and we entered. Silence filled the air as we rode down to the lobby.

Andre placed his hand at the back of my arm and guided me back to the car. He seemed genuinely caring.

In the car, I turned to him. "Seeing all of Vanessa's personal things made me try to imagine her life through her eyes." I took in a deep breath. "It was a little more than I could handle."

He listened without judgement and nodded. He

rested his hand atop mine and said, "It never gets any easier. I've seen much worst."

I was much calmer when he pulled the car in front of my building. There were no parking spots left. He unbuckled his seat belt.

"It's okay. I can let myself out."

He ignored my comment and came around to my side of the car to let me out.

"Thank you for lunch and getting me the interview with Ms. Rojas."

"It was my pleasure. Oh ... here." He pulled a card from his wallet and handed it to me. "Call me if you want to talk."

"Thank you."

"You *will* call me, right?"

I looked into his beautiful, caring eyes. "I might."

CHAPTER 3

She still played with dolls.

That danced though my head as I sat at my desk contemplating what I was going to write. I twisted a few strands of hair around my finger as I stared down at the recorder. *Coffee.* I'm going to need coffee to get through this.

I pushed away from the desk and padded down the long corridor passing a row of cubicles and Blackman's office. He wasn't in his office. I was relieved. I was halfway back to my desk when I heard the sound of Blackman's voice. "Watkins?"

I turned in his direction. "Yes."

"What do you have?"

"I'm on it. I'll get it to you soon." I hurried back to my desk as best I could without spilling any coffee.

I reclaimed my seat. The aroma of the freshly brewed coffee touched my nostrils. I blew over the steam and sipped. Not as good as the coffee from Midtown Bagels, but it would do.

I plugged in my earbuds to the recorder and listened to Ms. Rojas' story again. As I listened, my mind wandered off to those disturbing pictures that Andre had shown me in his office.

My hand trembled as I began to type:

She still played with dolls.

On the purple bed of sixteen-year-old murder victim, Vanessa Rojas, sit three ragdolls, each precisely lined up with her pillow in her purple decorated room. On her dresser rests shea butter lotion, a bottle of Guess Girl perfume, a clear plastic organizer filled with hair accessories, and a now-silent purple music box that plays "Swan Lake."

Vanessa had her whole life ahead of her until yesterday when someone raped and murdered her in her own bed.

When Vanessa looked out of her window the morning someone stole her life, what did she see? Did she see hope? Did she see a shining future?

Her mother Anna, a single mother of three, said Vanessa was a beloved daughter and loving big sister to her two younger brothers. She was a girl who loved animals and planned to be a veterinarian.

Did Vanessa see birds that day? Did she see people walking their dogs, dogs that might one day have been her future clients?

I then broke a cardinal rule of crime reporting: I inserted myself into the story because I couldn't help seeing her eyes in those pictures.

I looked through Vanessa's window and saw nothing but gloom today because a young woman with a royal purple future is no longer with us ...

My stomach was queasy. I pulled open the desk drawer and searched through the mess of loose envelopes, paperclips, pens, and sticky notes for the pack of gum I had thrown in last week. The minty flavor would calm my stomach. I unwrapped a stick and shoved it into my mouth, chewing twice as fast for quick relief before disposing of it.

I pressed my fingers back to the keyboard.

Who would steal such an innocent, caring girl from us? And why? The police report there was no sign of a break-in. Did Vanessa know her killer?

I lifted my coffee cup and took another sip. The warmth of the liquid going down my throat was calming.

As I continued listening to Ms. Rojas, my heart bled for her. Although she could no longer continue telling what she saw, the gruesome pictures told the rest. Multiple stab wounds all over this young girl's body. If that wasn't enough, the bastard also put his cigarette out on her as well. No mother should ever have to find her child this way.

I felt a teardrop roll down my cheek. I grabbed a Kleenex from the box in front of me. Janet appeared in front of my cubicle.

"Are you all right?" she asked.

"I'm fine. These damn allergies." I wiped my eyes.

"I'm on my way home. What about you? What time are you leaving?"

I glanced at my watch. "As soon as I'm done here. I have to submit this story I'm working on to Blackman before I leave." I faked a smile.

"What story is that?"

"It's a story about a young girl who was raped and murdered at the Lincoln Houses."

"I heard about that on the news. So sad. Don't let him keep you too late. I'll see you tomorrow."

"Good night."

As the hours passed and others filtered out of the office, I found myself re-writing the article for the fifth time. I had to get it right. I wanted to prove to Blackman that I was a journalist. A damn good one at that. This had been a challenging story that pushed me out of my comfort zone. Although my emotions were on a rollercoaster, I thought this was the type of journalism I wanted to do.

I re-read the final edit before pushing the send button on the email to Blackman.

I leaned my head back and closed my tired eyes. My desk phone rang, I saw that it was Blackman.

"Hello?"

"Watkins, don't leave yet. Give me a moment to look over your article."

Click

I kicked off my shoes, stood, and stretched my arms in the air. I reached for the coffee cup and contemplated whether or not I should get a refill. The phone rang again.

"Yes?"

"Nice job. Well done. It will tug thousands of heartstrings. It will be front page tomorrow."

Click

I stared at the phone. *I can't believe my ears! The world's grouchiest man gave me a compliment.*

I slid my feet back into my pumps and pulled my bag from the desk drawer. It slipped out of my grip and some of its contents spilled to the floor. I bent to pick them up. The last thing I picked up was Andre's card. *Detective Andre Moore, Homicide.* I sat down and stared at his card. I twirled it through my fingers as I drifted off thinking of how handsome he was.

I closed my eyes and remembered the touch of his strong hand at the back of my arm when he guided me across the street to get back into the car. Those beautiful dreamy hazel eyes as he stared at me while I questioned Ms. Rojas. The twinkle in his eyes when he smiled.

Nicole, girl, get a grip.

I dropped his card back into my bag.

Will we meet again, Detective Moore?

I giggled.

Damn, I hope so.

CHAPTER 4

I was *so* glad to be home in my apartment after a long and exhausting day.

Freddie, my cat, greeted me as I entered the door. I set my briefcase and purse on a nearby chair. He looked up at me, meowed, and circled his soft gray and black body around my leg. I bent down to pick him up and scratched him in the white area under his neck. "How are you, buddy? Did you miss Mommy?" He let out another soft meow. "Okay, let's get you something to eat."

I put him down gently, and he followed me into the kitchen, watching in anticipation while I opened a can of cat food and emptied it into his bowl. I scowled at the stack of mail on the counter that I had originally planned to go through tonight. I was too worn out to deal with bills, junk mail, and more bills.

Instead, I decided to run a warm bath to soak in and relax a little before turning in for the night. I poured a little of my favorite lavender oil into the bathwater—I love the smell of lavender and its soothing effect. Let's see ... what would go well with a warm soak? A glass of wine sounded good. While waiting for the tub to fill, I wrapped a towel around me and went into the kitchen to pour my glass of wine. There was a time when I strolled around the apartment stark naked. That was until Joann pointed out the pervert living in the building across from us who used his binoculars to peer into windows, watching women get undressed. I opened the refrigerator and took out the bottle of red wine that Joann had brought me back from her recent trip to Napa Valley, California.

I had met Joann about three years ago, several weeks after moving into this apartment building. I can still remember the first day we met—it was quite an eventful one.

I had just walked into my apartment building, exhausted from a full day of job interviews which had turned out to be unsuccessful. As soon as I entered, I saw water pooling in the kitchen. It was everywhere—all over the kitchen countertop and stovetop as well as the floor. I rushed to see where it was coming from. It was dripping from above, and when I looked up, I could see it seeping from the ceiling. The water had caused large blisters to form under the paint on one of the walls, and as the blisters descended, they left what looked like narrow tire tracks on the wall.

I hurried out of the kitchen and down the hall to the linen closet, pulled out several towels, and ran back into the kitchen, scattering towels all over the floor and using them to mop up the water. Then my doorbell rang. I wasn't expecting anyone, so I decided to ignore it and continued cleaning up the water, hoping whoever it was would just go away. I was in no mood for sales pitches.

The doorbell rang again. *Who could that be?* I remember also thinking that whoever it was, they had better have a very good reason for ringing my doorbell. I reluctantly stood, walked over to the door, and looked through the peephole. It was a woman. I opened the door slightly, and there stood a strikingly beautiful, tall, slender, caramel-colored woman in a tank top and yoga pants.

She looked at me and said, "Hi, my name is Joann Wesley. I live in the apartment below you. There's water dripping from my kitchen ceiling, and I thought that I'd come check to see if the leak was coming from this apartment."

Surprisingly, she didn't appear to be upset at all over it. If I hadn't been having such a bad day to begin with, it might have been a laughable situation. I offered a small smile as I extended my hand and said, "Nice to meet you. Joann. My name is Nicole Watkins. It appears we're having the same problem."

"Really?"

"Come in ... let me show you what I'm talking about," I said as I stepped back to open the door wider.

We walked a few steps over to the kitchen. As we entered, she glanced down at the soaked towels sprawled across the floor. I immediately pointed to the huge spot on the ceiling where water had been leaking through.

She looked up to where I was pointing. Mouth agape, she turned to me. "Wow. I wonder what could have caused that to happen. Well, before I came up here, I stopped at the super's apartment to let him know about the water in my apartment. I knocked on his door, but no one answered, so I wrote a note and slipped it under his door. I didn't have nearly as much come through as you did, though. How long has this been going on?" She followed me as I picked the wet towels up from the kitchen floor and took them into the bathroom, throwing them into the bathtub.

I stopped at the closet to gather more towels to finish mopping up the water from the floor. I sighed. "I have no idea how long. I just walked in the door—literally a few minutes before you rang the doorbell—and found water everywhere."

Joann grabbed some towels from my hands as we returned to the kitchen. "Let me help you clean up this mess."

She kneeled to sop up the remaining water from the floor, and I took care of the walls and countertops. The dripping from the ceiling had finally subsided. I thanked her for helping me and as she was about to leave, she turned and asked, "Why don't we both go upstairs and let them know about the water leak? Maybe they don't realize that it's affecting two other units."

I stared at her for an awkward moment before responding because all I really wanted to do was shower and go to bed after an exhausting day, but I owed her at least that much for helping me clean up the mess—and it was also the right thing to do. *Ugh.*

"Okay, let's go," I said, trying not to let my reluctance show.

When we reached the apartment above my unit, the door was partially open. Joann knocked on the door, and we both shouted simultaneously, "Hello in there!"

The superintendent of the building, a short, stocky Polish man who appeared to be in his fifties came to the door with a wrench in his hand, apparently already in the midst of making repairs. He seemed quite annoyed to be disturbed. Frowning, he looked at us without uttering a word.

"Hi, we're sorry to disturb you, but we came up to let someone know that water coming from this apartment was leaking down into both our apartments," Joann said as she shifted her feet.

He grimaced. "Yeah, I figured—that's why I'm here fixing the problem. I'll check on the units below tomorrow." He shut the door before we had a chance to respond.

Joann and I looked at each other and laughed. Heading down the stairway back to our own apartments, Joann suddenly realized that she didn't have the keys to her apartment—she had mistakenly left them in mine. Once inside my place, she found them sitting on the kitchen countertop where she had left them. We chatted for a few minutes before she left. I found out that she was also not a native New Yorker. She had been born and raised in San Francisco, California. Her parents still lived in the state, and she flew out to visit them often. She had completed both her undergraduate and graduate degrees at New York University a few years ago, had fallen in love with New York City, and decided to remain there and make it her home.

Joann was a free spirit. She was one of the few

people who had won me over from the very beginning. She always seemed to find the best in people. She had worked as a stockbroker for a few years on Wall Street, making an impressive salary, but one day she decided that she had had enough of the stress that came along with being a stockbroker on Wall Street, and she quit her job. She said that she had always wanted to teach yoga, so shortly after quitting her Wall Street job, she opened up a yoga studio. She loved it and never regretted her decision. Somehow I could never picture Joann as some hotshot Wall Street broker, wearing a skirt suit every day.

I submerged myself into the bathtub. The warmth of the water soothed my skin, and a sense of calmness blanketed my whole being. I reached for the glass of wine I had previously placed on the tiled edge of the tub and took a sip of it, savoring it for a few seconds and enjoying its delicious, smooth and crisp taste before swallowing. *I must thank Joann for choosing such a great-tasting pinot noir.* I'm no wine connoisseur, but this was some good stuff.

After taking a few more sips of wine, I put a bath pillow behind my head, leaned back against the tub, and shut my eyes, the memories of the day dancing through my head. I found myself still curious about the sadness that had washed over Andre while discussing some of the case details. What was he holding back? And what were the odds of me finding out? I could ask for a second interview, saying I'm doing a follow-up on the story. Not a bad idea, but the problem would be getting Blackman on board—probably a lost cause. He seemed more interested in fresh news, not follow-up stories. The only way he would give approval would be if there was a break in the investigation.

My thoughts then wandered to being in the car with Andre, studying him discreetly in my peripheral vision—and sometimes stealing a deliberate glance. I had watched as he took control of the car, navigating in and out of traffic, his strong, manly hands gripping the steering wheel. I imagined the feel of those hands gently caressing my body. Just the thought of it made me warm all over.

The bath water was starting to cool. I stepped out of the tub and waited as the water drained, then took a quick shower to rinse the residue of bath oil from my body.

Freddie was curled up at the bottom of my bed, already asleep when I entered the bedroom. I slid under the sheet and comforter and closed my eyes, thoughts of Andre wafting through my mind as I fell asleep ...

A dark figure is looming over me, but I can't make

out whom it is. He looks angry. I attempt to scream, and
he strikes my mouth hard with his fist. My mouth throbs,
and I can taste the blood as it trickles down my throat. He
covers my mouth with his hand, sealing it hard and tight.
His grip is hurting me. I try to scramble free, but my body
seems paralyzed. I can't move. Oh God, he's going to kill
me! Please don't let him kill me! My heart is racing. He
takes a soft, spongy object and stuffs it in my mouth hard
to smother any sounds I might try to make. I can't breathe.
He pins my arms above my head with one hand and uses
his free hand to push my silk nightgown up, aggressively
ripping off my panties. Somebody help me! Please! I can
feel teardrops sliding from the corners of my eyes. He
pushes my legs apart with his knee and forces himself
inside me. He thrusts inside me—harder and deeper. My
vagina is on fire from the friction. He doesn't speak at all,
but grunts as he relieves himself inside me. I still can't
move. My arms and legs feel like dead weight. He reaches
behind him and grabs something. I can see it in his hand
now. A shiny object reflecting the dim light shining
through the window. He brings it closer. Oh my God, it's a
knife! He raises it in the air, about to plunge it into me—

I woke up in a cold sweat, shivering and gasping
for air as I bolted upright in bed. Freddie meowed
loudly and leaped off the bed onto the floor and
scatted out of the room. I sat there for a few minutes,
shaking and feeling discombobulated because I

realized that I had been dreaming about the murder victim, Vanessa—but in my dream, *I* was the person being raped and tortured. I felt my throat getting tight and dry and got out of bed to get a glass of water from the kitchen. Freddie was nowhere in sight. Shakily, I held the glass of water in my hand, bringing it to my mouth to take a sip. I had never been so afraid in my life. Setting the glass on the counter, I immediately checked all the windows to be sure they were closed and locked. I also checked the double lock on the door leading into my apartment.

Too nervous and shaken to go back to bed, I picked up my cell phone to call Joann. I needed to talk to someone to calm my nerves. The time on my cell phone read 1:30 a.m.—Joann would be asleep. No sense in alarming her over nothing.

I set my cell phone down on the kitchen counter and walked over to the chair where my briefcase rested. Opening it, I pulled out Andre's business card. I tapped the edge of the card on my hand several times, contemplating whether or not to give him a call. Flipping it over, I saw that he had handwritten his private cell phone number on the back of it. *Hmm ... interesting. I got my wish.* Why had I been drawn to his card? What was I thinking? What could I possibly say to this man at 1:30 in the morning? *Hello, it's me, Nicole. I just had a dream about the killer.* I quickly pushed the thought of calling Andre out of my head and put the card back in my briefcase.

I ran my hand through my hair, trying to figure out what else I could do to calm myself. I decided to stay up and watch TV. I grabbed the big colorful afghan blanket that Mom had made for me a couple of years ago from the closet and draped it over me while I lay on the sofa. It felt comforting being wrapped up in it. For some reason, it made me think of how when I was a little girl and got frightened, Mom and Dad would come into my room to make sure I was okay. Mom would lie down on the bed next to me until I fell asleep again.

I reached for the remote and turned on the TV. I didn't care what was on—I was willing to watch anything that would keep me from falling back into that nightmare. Flipping through a few channels, I landed on the game show, *Family Feud*. Maybe answering along with the contestants would keep my mind busy. But it was weird—and annoying—how every time a contestant gave an answer that clearly did not make sense, the rest of the family shouted, "Good answer," so I changed my mind and settled on watching a repeat of the movie *Sleepless in Seattle*. I had always been a sucker for love stories, and that one happened to be one of my favorites.

Freddie reappeared and nestled on my lap as I lay stretched on the sofa. My eyes started to feel heavy, and I drifted off to a restless sleep, haunted by the face of a sixteen-year-old girl.

CHAPTER 5

It had been several weeks since my interview with Detective Andre Moore. Yes, I was back to referring to him by his title. I couldn't bring myself to continue calling him Andre. In hindsight, I should have given him a follow-up call to thank him for the interview. *Hmm ... still may not be such a bad idea.* The information that I obtained from the interview with him had really helped show off my skills as a journalist, and Blackman was still impressed with my article on the rape and murder of Vanessa Rojas, so impressed he assigned me to several other high-profile murder cases in Brooklyn and Staten Island. I was so relieved I hadn't screwed up my first story, especially since there had been times I was seriously distracted by Detective Moore.

The day after my nightmare, I went to work feeling like I had been run over by an eighteen-wheeler. I was bone tired and aching all over from falling asleep on my lumpy sofa. I had overslept because I didn't hear the alarm clock beeping from the bedroom. When I finally awakened, I had dragged myself off the sofa and into the shower. Coffee would have normally given me a quick boost of energy, but it didn't seem to do the job that morning. Thank goodness Blackman was still in good spirits over my article—otherwise, I may have been on the chopping block for arriving to work an hour late. A few coworkers complimented me, giving me the thumbs up.

Janice, my cube neighbor and friend—a petite redhead with a bubbly personality—was smiling brightly. "Good job, Nikki! We have to go out and celebrate."

And, of course, in the midst of all the well-wishers, there had to be a jerk—aka Stanley Pittman. He sneered as he walked past my cubicle. I politely gave him the finger with a devious grin on my face. Janice looked flabbergasted at my gesture, but I couldn't help myself. The man simply brought out the worst in me.

Though the new murder cases were exciting, the Vanessa Rojas case continued to haunt me, but so far, there had been no news of any breaks in the investigation.

My social life, however, had been boring. I hadn't dated much since I divorced that cheating bastard,

Michael. It still pained me to think of the day I had walked in on him and Sandra, my so-called good friend, fucking in our bed of all places. I had been beyond devastated. I had just stood motionless in the doorway, frozen in shock. I dropped whatever I held in my hand, which made a sound loud enough to get their attention. They had both seemed quite surprised to see me standing there. The good thing was that the S.O.B. certainly could not deny his cheating, which worked to my advantage when I filed for the divorce. Once the shock wore off, I threw them both out and filed the following day.

****

My cell phone rang as I was about to take a sip from the glass of wine that I'd ordered while waiting for Janice and Joann to arrive at Sassy's, the bar and grill where we had agreed to meet.

"Hi, Joann," I answered, seeing her name on the caller ID.

"Hi, Nikki! I just wanted to let you know that I should be there in about fifteen minutes. I'm trying to find parking, and you know how that can be in the city."

I had learned that while New York City consisted of five boroughs—Brooklyn, Queens, Bronx, Staten Island and Manhattan—most people living there referred to Manhattan as "the city."

More patrons seemed to have flowed into the restaurant. I didn't expect Janice for at least another thirty minutes because she was stuck at work on a project with a deadline. I took my glass of wine from the bar and was about to get the three of us a table when I felt a tap on my shoulder. I turned to see who it was and nearly lost my balance when I saw Detective Andre Moore standing there with a big grin on his beautiful face.

"Hello, Nicole."

Damn, this man is fine! He was wearing dark denim pants and a short-sleeved, button-down dress shirt that exposed a portion of his biceps. My heart skipped a beat.

"Uh, Detective …"

"Oh … so we're once again back to that?" he said, still grinning. "How've you been?"

"Great," I responded. "What brings you here?"

"I ended my shift early. Was driving by and thought I'd come in for a little down time." With a raised brow, he asked, "What brings *you* here?"

"I'm meeting a couple of friends." I glanced over at the entrance door, checking for Janice or Joann. "I was just going to get us a table."

He stared at me and asked, "Would you mind if I kept you company until your friends show up?"

I swallowed, not knowing how to respond. There

was a connection between us that I couldn't quite explain. Having him next to me was driving my hormones insane. Even when I had first started dating that asshole Michael—and was still sweet on him—I had never felt this strong a charge. *Maybe it's just lust. It's been a while since I've been this physically attracted to a man.*

"Uh ... sure." *Why am I agreeing to this? And why do I seem to lose all control around this man?*

A waiter appeared and led us to a table. Andre sat right beside me! *The nerve!* Once we seated ourselves, the waiter smiled and pulled out his pen and pad, asking if he could get us anything to start with. I told him we were waiting on two other people. Andre waited for me to finish and then asked for a glass of water.

"Nicole, I don't know exactly how to say this, so I'm just going to come right out with it."

I looked at him, puzzled.

"Since that day you showed up in my office, I haven't been able to get you out of my mind. I know this may sound lame, but it's the truth. I thought about calling you—a few times—but I wasn't sure of what I'd say to you if you answered." He searched my face, waiting for a response.

I had just taken another sip of my wine as he began to talk. It must have gone down the wrong way because I started choking and trying to catch my breath.

He came around to my side of the table, put his hand on my back, and gave it a few gentle pats. "Are you all right?"

"Yes, I'm fine. I think it went down the wrong way." I cleared my throat.

I repeated in my head what I'd heard him say—"*Since that day that you showed up in my office, I can't seem to get you out of my mind.*" I was still unsure of how to respond.

"How do you feel about what I just told you?" he asked as his eyes widened.

"I'm not quite sure how to respond."

"Nicole, I know you're just as attracted to me as I am to you." He stared at me with those beautiful hazel eyes which seemed to have darkened a bit.

I could feel the heat of my body turning up a notch. I fanned myself and glanced around, hoping to see either Janice or Joann, and spotted them sitting at the bar, looking in my direction and grinning. I glared at them, wondering how long they had been sitting there. It was obvious that they didn't want to interrupt what they thought might have been going on between Andre and me. They must have figured out who I was sitting with since

I had described Andre to them in great detail on several occasions.

"It looks like my friends have arrived," I said happily, changing the topic.

He glanced in the direction of my glare. He smirked and waved to Joann and Janice.

They both waved back.

"It also looks like they want to give us some alone time," Andre said.

Feeling defeated, I succumbed. I relaxed my shoulders, sat back, and accepted the fact that I would be in the company of Detective Moore—without my notepad as a crutch to divert my attention from my feelings.

"Are you going to deny your attraction?"

"Listen, Andre ... you're a very attractive man, and I don't know of any woman in her right mind who wouldn't be attracted to you ... but I'm just not ready for this," I explained. *Why am I not ready for this? I must be losing my mind. Look at this gorgeous, sexy man.*

He had moved closer and closer to me since his attempted rescue, his knee occasionally brushing mine. He stared at me for a moment with an intensity that was both sexy and hypnotic. Leaning in, he brought his hand to my face and held it softly, bringing it closer to his. He brushed his lips against mine. I parted my mouth, and he slid his tongue in, deepening the kiss. Our tongues intertwined, dancing seductively as we tasted one another. I followed his lead and took his tongue in deeper. He groaned, pulling me closer to him. My head was spinning. He ended the kiss and backed away.

"I guess I have my answer," he said, smiling.

"I don't know about this, Andre. I mean, you seem like a nice guy and all, but—"

"Nicole, I promise I won't hurt you. There's something about you that's captivating to me. I feel we were meant to meet, meant to be together. I can't explain it."

The waiter returned to our table, looking as though he thought he was interrupting. "Do you need more time for your party to arrive, or are you ready to order?"

I hadn't thought about food since I sat down. Andre looked at me and asked if he could make a suggestion. My mind was overflowing with so many thoughts—and food was not one of them. I nodded, agreeing to let him order for us. He ordered smoked salmon, pilaf, and garlic spinach. It sounded delicious.

"Nicole? May I ask you a question? You don't have to answer if you don't feel comfortable."

"What do you want to know?" I asked, twisting the napkin that lay across my lap.

"Who hurt you?"

I glanced away for a second, contemplating whether I wanted to reveal that part of my life to him. *Am I that transparent? Is it stamped on my forehead? If I avoid the question, he'll suspect I'm hiding something. If I get defensive—same outcome. Damn him for putting me on the spot like this!*

"It's not a matter of whether I've been hurt," I explained. "Life is uncomplicated for me right now, and I would like it to stay that way."

The waiter returned with our meals. We ate silently for a few moments. Although I wasn't hungry, the food was delicious. I was quite impressed that he had been able to choose a dish I would enjoy eating.

"This is really good," I said as I put another forkful of rice in my mouth.

He reached for my free hand and tucked it between both his hands.

I swear, I felt like my heart was going to jump out of my chest.

"I want to apologize for overstepping my boundaries earlier. I just wanted to assure you that I would never hurt you. Will you please give me a chance?"

My brain and heart battled as I tried to come to a decision. I bit my lip. "Andre, it's true that I've been hurt before. Deeply hurt. And it's taken me quite a bit of time to get over it. I'm still a work in progress when it comes to trust, and I don't want to bring any old baggage into a new relationship. It wouldn't be fair."

"I'm a very patient man, Nicole. I know that trust has to be earned. Even if you hadn't been hurt before, my trust would still have to be earned. I know it will take time, but I would just like the chance to prove to you that you can trust me."

"I don't think I can make that kind of decision right here, right now."

He leaned in and kissed my forehead softly. "It's all right, I won't push you. Take some time to think about it."

I appreciatively mouthed, "Thank you."

"Have you dated since your divorce?"

"It's been three years. Yes. I've dated here and there, but nothing serious." I poked at the salmon. "How about you?"

He sipped from his glass of water. "If you're asking when was my last relationship... I'll have to say about eighteen months ago."

"Really?"

"Why is that unbelievable?"

"It's not that it is unbelievable, I figured a guy as handsome as you are would have been swept up by now," I smiled.

"Touché."

The waiter returned. "Can I get you anything else?"

Andre said no and I shook my head.

"So what happened?" I asked.

"Hmm ... where do I begin? Long story short, she couldn't deal with what I did for a living or the long hours my job sometimes require."

"Your work seems interesting. Have you always wanted to be a cop?"

"You seem more interesting than my work." He moved in closer.

I moved closer to him, too, but I had completely forgotten about Janice and Joann until they both walked over to tell me that they were ready to leave. I introduced them to Andre. He stood up to shake hands with each of them.

Joann offered him a smile. "Nice to meet you, Detective. We've heard so much about you." She glanced at me and winked.

Janice nodded, grinning widely. They both seemed taken by Andre's good looks and charm.

"The pleasure is all mine, ladies. I hope they were

good things that you heard." He gave them a warm smile and winked at me.

What's with all the winking? I felt a little embarrassed. I didn't want Andre to know I'd been discussing him with my friends.

Janice turned to me. "Nikki, are you leaving with us or are you staying a while longer?"

I was about to respond when Andre interrupted. "Nicole, stay a bit longer. I'll take you home."

It was more of a statement than a question. I looked at my two friends for a moment. They both gave a nod, indicating I should stay.

I smiled at them. "I'll give you both a call later."

****

Although the days had gotten progressively hotter, the nights were still cool. As we rode in his late model sleek black Audi across the 59th Street Bridge into Queens, there was a gentle breeze passing through the open windows. The air felt good against my face. *How could he afford such a nice ride on a cop's salary?* I turned toward Andre, and he was looking so magnificently handsome, even in the darkness of the car. He must have felt me looking at him because he reached over and took my hand. He caressed it for a moment before bringing it to his mouth and planting a soft kiss upon it.

"I had a great evening with you, Nicole—or should I call you Nikki?" He grinned.

"Most of my friends call me Nikki, but I really like the way you say Nicole."

"Is that right?"

"Yes," I murmured.

He turned toward me, smiling broadly.

After parking the car near my apartment building, Andre insisted on escorting me to my door to make sure I got in safely. I couldn't determine if this was him being a gentleman, him being a policeman, or him thinking he was going to get laid. I have to admit, I was glad that he offered to walk me to my door. It had been such an awesome evening, and quite frankly, I was not ready for it to end. When we reached the door to my apartment, I handed him the key to unlock the door. As we entered, Freddie greeted us with a soft meow. Andre stiffened, seeming a bit surprised. It was obvious he hadn't expected to see a cat—or any other moving object, for that matter.

"I apologize for not warning you about Freddie."

It was a good thing I had left a couple of lights on in the apartment or Freddie might have been toast.

"Do you have pets?" I asked.

With his back to me, he kneeled down and stroked Freddie's head. "I had a dog, but I had to give him to a friend because my work took up too much of my time." He stood and faced me.

"Would you like to stay for a little while?" I asked nervously.

He closed the distance between us, put his arms around my waist, and pulled me closer to him. I felt his hardness pressed against me. He gazed into my eyes and whispered, "I thought you'd never ask."

I stepped back from his embrace to catch my breath a moment and wrap my head around what was happening.

He looked puzzled, cocking his head to the side. "What's wrong?"

I tried to look calm—and act calm—but inside I was a bundle of nerves. I wanted this gorgeous man so badly that I honestly felt my clit throbbing with desire. "Nothing's wrong ... I just wanted to step back and take a good look at you."

"Hmm ... I hope you like what you see," he murmured.

"Do you want something to eat or drink?" I asked, walking toward the kitchen. I needed to put some distance between us. As I fumbled with the teapot on the stove, he came up from behind and put his arms around me. I felt him pressing against me. He gently pulled my hair aside and kissed softly up and down my neck. *Mercy!*

He kissed my earlobe softly, nibbling on it, and then turned me to face him. He wrapped both arms around me, and I did the same to him. His lips brushed mine, his tongue tasted my lips, and I parted my mouth and allowed his tongue to slide inside. His hands moved slowly down my back to rest on my butt. He caressed it, making slow circling motions. He released my mouth and kissed down my neck.

I moaned softly. My nipples were hard and sensitive, and I could feel the moistness between my legs. I took him by the hand and led him down the hall to my bedroom. We began kissing passionately again, long and lingering. I began unbuttoning his shirt until his chest was exposed. Gliding my hand over his hard, muscled chest, I slid his shirt off completely. I began kissing his bare chest, softly and tenderly.

He, in turn, pulled my blouse over my head. As he unhooked my bra and slid it off, my breasts sprang free. He cupped them in his hands, caressing and kissing them softly and gently tugging one nipple at a time with his mouth.

As he rolled my nipples between his fingers, I felt as if I was going to explode. I felt myself getting wetter.

He lowered me to the bed, running his tongue lightly across one of my nipples before putting his warm, moist mouth on it and nibbling. He moved his hand down my body, sliding it under my skirt and pulling my panties to the side. With his fingers, he stroked teasingly over me before entering me. I moaned and circled my hips, begging for him.

He whispered in my ear, "You're so wet ... I want you so much ... but if you're not ready, and this is too soon, let me know, and I'll stop."

Is he freaking kidding me? Why on earth would I want this to stop?

"I want you, too! Please! Don't stop!" *Oh my goodness, he smells and feels so good.*

He sat up and slid my skirt down over my hips. I lifted them so that he could pull it off completely. He pulled my panties down, kissing my inner thighs as he did so, it was electrifying. I lay there completely naked. He removed his pants and his underwear as our eyes locked. I couldn't help but stare at his hard on. He was well-endowed, and I licked my lips in anticipation as he moved closer, lowering his body onto mine. He groaned and covered my mouth, his slick tongue deep inside, tasting me passionately. My heart was running a marathon. I wanted him inside me so badly. He slid a finger into my wetness and teased my throbbing clit, stroking it as he continued to devour my mouth. My body rippled with pleasure.

He entered me slowly, and our bodies synched.

He stared down at me, breathing harder, pulling out a bit and then plunging back into me, quickening his pace.

I screamed out in total ecstasy as I came, my body trembling. He plunged into me again, head tilted back, spurting his cum into me as I exploded with another orgasm.

Did I really just come twice? Oh God! He probably thinks I'm a freak!

"That was intense," he whispered. "I'm sorry I didn't, um, last very long."

I barely lasted a minute! Three years is entirely too long to go without sex! "It was ... it was great. Will you ... no, I don't have a right to ask this."

"Go ahead."

"Will you stay the night with me?"

He pulled me close and kissed my shoulder. "I was hoping you would ask."

As we lay naked in each other's arms and drifted off to sleep, I had good dreams all night because a dream of a man was beside me.

CHAPTER 6

I sat at my desk, fanning myself with an empty file folder trying to keep cool in the summer heat.

The air conditioning had stopped working in parts of the building and, unfortunately, our office was one of those affected. Sweat had begun to bead on my face and down my neck, and I only needed a few more minutes to finish proofreading an article about a well-known therapist who had been sexually abusing patients while under hypnosis before I submitted it to Blackman for approval and left the office in search of a much cooler environment.

My cell phone vibrated with a call. I could tell it was Andre by the picture I had assigned to his number. Since that night in my apartment, we had begun seeing each other on a regular basis. He made me feel like no other man had ever made me feel before—both sexually and spiritually. I felt free to express who I was as a woman when I was with him. Through him, I had learned to trust again.

"Hello," I answered with a big grin.

"Hey, babe," he said, sending shivers down my spine.

My body's response to this man never seemed to dim.

"My father and his wife are having a wedding anniversary celebration," Andre said, "and I would love for you to come with me."

This is a little weird. He's never mentioned anything about his parents before. Wait a minute—did he say his father's wife? Is that how he refers to his mother? Hmm ... interesting.

"I'd love to go. Will we have to leave New York?"

"No. They live on Long Island. They'll be celebrating their fifteenth wedding anniversary."

"Fifteenth anniversary?" I choked out.

"I'll explain that later," he replied.

"When will it take place? I mean, what day?" *Why was it only their fifteen-year anniversary?*

"It's supposed to be this coming Saturday around six p.m.," he said. "I'll call you with the details later. I just wanted to see if you'd come along with me."

"Sounds great. I'm looking forward to it. Andre?"

"Yes?"

"Can you at least tell me whether I should dress formally or casually?"

"You ladies kill me with that" He laughed. "It'll be held at their home. I'm sure you'll look beautiful in whatever you wear. I'll call you later."

I spent the next few minutes reading through my article one final time before forwarding it to Blackman. I stood up and peeked around Janice's cubicle to see if she had already left for home. My intention was to persuade her into a little shopping this afternoon. Saturday was only two days away, and I needed something nice to wear to Andre's parents' wedding anniversary celebration. Although I had a good sense of fashion, I wanted a second opinion on what to wear for this special occasion, especially since it would be my first time meeting Andre's family. I could definitely use Janice's help with this task. She had such a flair for fashion and always looked so refined and chic. She could have easily been a fashion model if she were taller. It would be great to get her take on a few outfits.

Her back was to me in her cubicle as she gathered her belongings.

"Knock, knock," I said, grinning slyly and trying not to startle her.

She turned, surprised. "What are you still doing here? I thought you left."

"I needed to proof my article before handing it in to Blackman." I leaned my shoulder against the entrance wall to her cubicle and cocked my head to one side. "Do you have any plans right now?"

She narrowed her eyes. "I'm afraid to ask why."

"Why are you looking at me that way?" I laughed. "Well ... I was wondering if you would like to come shopping with me."

"Oh, uh ... I'm not really in the mood for trying on clothes, Nikki. You know how you get when we go shopping." She rolled her eyes.

I have the strange habit of having my friends try on the same outfit as I do so that I can get a feel for how it actually looks on another human being and not just on me in my reflection in the mirror. I've been doing it since high school, and it drives my friends crazy. Hence, the reason for Janice's reluctance to go shopping with me.

"I promise I won't ask you to do that. Besides, I don't have time for that today." I chuckled.

"Hmm ... are you sure?"

"Yes, I'm sure."

"All right, I'm going to hold you to that."

We vacated our desks and headed for the elevator. Just my luck—when we reached the elevators, none other than the creep, Stanley Pittman, was also waiting. It seemed that I was constantly running into him at the elevator. If we weren't on the fourteenth floor of the building, I would have taken the stairs to avoid him.

"Ms. Watkins, Ms. Kent," he said smugly.

Janice nodded.

I refused to look at him—I didn't want to become nauseous.

When the doors to the elevator opened, that arrogant S.O.B. didn't even have the decency to allow us into the elevator before him.

Janice glanced at me and snickered.

I rolled my eyes.

We exited the building into the muggy summer heat. It felt like at least 100 degrees. As we strolled down the crowded sidewalk heading toward the subway station, Janice asked, "Is there some special reason why you're shopping for clothes in the middle of the week?"

"It's not the middle of the week—it's Thursday," I corrected her, smiling mischievously.

"Whatever. So you're not going to tell me why?"

I studied her a moment. I didn't want her to read more into Andre's invitation than what it was. Both Joann and Janice already had me walking down the aisle with him.

"I've been invited to a wedding anniversary celebration on Saturday," I explained nonchalantly.

"Whose wedding anniversary?"

"Andre's parents," I said, trying to avoid eye contact with her because I knew what was coming next. When she didn't promptly respond, I glanced at her suspiciously.

"Oh, really ... you're going to meet his *parents?*" She raised an eyebrow in delight.

"Janice," I said with a frown. "Let's not go there."

"Not another word." She giggled, using her thumb and forefinger to glide across her lips as if zipping them shut.

The subway station was as hot and muggy as it had been above ground. We were shoved into the subway car as the doors opened. Although the subway car was crammed with people, at least there was air conditioning. I almost hated to get out of the train when it pulled into the 34th Street-Herald Square station—our exit. We made our way off the packed train and back onto another crowded street.

We browsed a couple of boutiques in Midtown but couldn't find anything that caught our eyes, so we headed to Macy's on 34th Street. The store was packed with people in almost every section visible from where we stood.

I loved Macy's and the rush I got each time I entered it—especially around the Christmas holidays with all of the beautiful Christmas decorations and displays throughout the store. And each year, there was a different window display theme—along with the classic *Miracle on 34th Street* theme. On my first visit to the store around Christmas three years ago, I was totally mesmerized by the decorations, the window displays, the crowds of people flowing in and out of the store—as well as the grandness of the store itself. Although I felt lonely in a big city where I didn't know anyone, I also felt—strange as it was—as if it was where I belonged. My thoughts were interrupted when Janice nudged me.

"Let the shopping begin. Will it be dress casual or formal?"

"I'm not sure. Andre says that the celebration is being held at his parents' house. Why don't we look through *both* sections?"

We searched through endless rows of dresses. I tried on six different dresses. Janice shook her head at two, frowned on two others, and gave the thumbs up on the last two dresses I tried on. We finally agreed upon a beautiful strapless cocktail dress made of peach silk chiffon, the peach perfectly complementing my olive skin tone and long dark hair.

I was starting to feel sweaty. Maybe it was all the pulling off and putting on dresses, but when Janice said that she was also feeling hot, I knew it must have been the air conditioning in the store or lack of it.

As we strolled along the aisles making our way to the cashier, the lights flickered then went out.

The entire store was dark.

I grabbed Janice's arm, and my heart raced.

"It's just another rolling blackout, Nicole," Janice said. "Nothing to worry about."

It was easy for her to say.

She didn't have bad dreams every time she closed her eyes in the dark.

CHAPTER 7

I had just stepped out of the shower when I heard the doorbell ring. *I wonder who that could be.* It was far too early for Andre to arrive to take me to his parents' house. I wrapped myself in a long bath towel and grabbed another towel to wrap my dripping wet hair as I walked down the hall to answer the door. I looked through the peephole to see Joann standing there, fully dressed in running gear. *I was supposed to be doing a 5K run with her today!*

When I opened the door, she looked at me expectantly. "Why aren't you dressed yet?" she asked.

Oh Lord, how could I have forgotten about this? I was completely speechless. I swallowed hard.

"Nikki, please tell me that you didn't forget about our run today," she said as she stepped into the apartment.

"Joann, I am *so* sorry. I didn't mean to ... Please forgive me?"

She waved her hand. "It's fine. Just go hurry and get dressed—we still have time to make it."

"Joann, I completely forgot about the run when Andre asked me to go with him to his parents' wedding anniversary celebration today," I murmured.

"Say what?" she sputtered. "You're going to meet his parents today? Nikki, that's great!"

"Wait a minute! Hold your horses! It's not like that at all. It's just an invitation to an anniversary thing. That's it."

"Um-hum, okay, whatever you say," she said with a devious grin. "So what are you wearing? Are you nervous?" She followed me to my bedroom.

"Of course, I'm nervous! The weird thing is he'd never mentioned anything about his parents until the other day when he invited me to this celebration. The other weird thing is he says it's their *fifteenth* wedding anniversary." I walked over to the closet and took out my new dress.

"Hmm ... fifteen years. That's weird. Maybe this isn't his father's first wife."

"That's what I was thinking, too."

She took the dress out of my hand and held it up in the air. "This dress is beautiful. You're going to look absolutely gorgeous."

"Janice helped me pick it out. I convinced her to

go shopping with me after work to look for a dress."
I laughed.

"You're kidding! Did you make her try it on, too?
You know how you are." She laughed heartily.

"No. She made me promise not to ask her to try
on anything before we even left to go shopping—but
there were many times I was tempted to ask her.
Speaking of which, since you and I are the same size,
why don't you try it on now so that I can see what it
looks like on you?" I smiled slyly.

"Look at the time! I need to get going if I'm going
to make it to the starting line on time." She tapped
the face of her watch as she walked toward the door.

"Oh c'mon, it'll only take a second," I pleaded.

Looking over her shoulder, she said, "I hope you
have a wonderful time today. Don't worry about a
thing—you're going to be gorgeous! I look forward
to hearing all about it. *Ciao*."

I shook my head, smiling, and bent down to pick
up Freddie.

"Hey buddy, I guess I'm on my own with this
one."

He meowed softly and snuggled his head against
my chin.

I returned to my closet to see what shoes would
work with the dress. After trying on several pairs, I
decided on a pair of nude peep-toe pumps. I put the

shoes on and held the dress close to my body. *Perfect.*
I pulled my hair up, trying to decide if I wanted to
wear it swept up or flowing with a few curls.
Decisions, decisions. I started to put the shoes back in
the closet when my telephone rang. My parents had
convinced me to get a landline phone in case of any
electricity outages from storms, hurricanes, or any
other natural disaster that might come up. Although
I hardly ever used the phone, it did come in handy
when my cell phone was dead. And it was always the
number my parents seemed to use to call me.

"Hello?" I answered, not knowing which one of
them was on the other end.

"Hello, honey, how are you?" my mother
responded cheerfully.

"Hi, Mom. I'm doing great."

"Your father and I were just talking about how
we haven't heard from you in a while, and we were
wondering if everything was okay with you,
darling," she said in her sweet southern drawl.

"Mom, I'm fine. We talked just two weeks ago."
I looked up into the air. My mother could be a little
dramatic at times. "There's no need to worry. I'm
fine. I promise."

"Yes, darling, but we still worry about you up
there in that big city all by yourself."

"We've gone through this before, Mom. I'm not

a child—I can take care of myself. Besides, I have friends. I'm not alone."

"Nikki, do you remember the Carsons who lived in that big mansion on Pine Street?" This woman switched subjects so often, it was hard to keep up with her at times.

"Yes, Mom. What about the Carsons?"

"Well, their oldest son, Stephen, who lives in California, was home visiting last week. He's a plastic surgeon for some of the stars in Hollywood."

I think I know where she is going with this. "That's nice, Mom. I'm sure he's a good surgeon."

"Honey, he asked about you," she said joyfully.

"Mother," I scolded softly.

"What? It's been three years now since your divorce. Don't you think that you should be courting now?"

I did not wish to have this conversation. I wondered if I should mention Andre to her. Maybe that would get her off my back for a while. On the other hand, it could open up a whole new can of worms. *If I don't say something, she's going to keep shoving this Stephen down my throat.* My mom was tenacious when it came to these things. When I visited my parents six months ago, she set me up on a blind date with a friend's nerdy son—who also happened to be a doctor. To appease her I went out

81

to dinner with him, and I've regretted it ever since. He showed up wearing a bow tie with his hair greased back. He wore pants that hung just above his ankles. I was showered with spit whenever he talked. At dinner, he spilled soup all over himself. His idea of conversation was talking nonstop about the same boring subject over and over again—he went on and on about his research project for finding a vaccine to cure birds of the flu. When the date ended, and he brought me back home, he leaned in and attempted to kiss me with his crusty lips. I backed away and offered him my hand instead. Even that repulsed me. But growing up southern, I had deeply instilled, good manners. It creeped me out just thinking about it.

"Mom, I'm, um, I'm dating someone," I said.

"Huh? What did you say, honey? Did you say that you were courting?"

"I said that I am dating someone."

She yelled out to my dad in excitement while still holding the telephone, "Lawrence, honey! Nikki is dating someone! Did you hear me, dear? Our daughter is dating!"

I winced at the loudness of her voice. My dad is not as dramatic as she is. I heard him mumble something, but I couldn't make out what he said.

"Nikki, who is this young fellow, and what does

he do? Have you met his parents yet? Is he a city fellow?"

"Mom, I will tell you all about him another time. But I need to get dressed because he's picking me up shortly."

"Nikki, I want to know about this man. Can you at least tell me his name? What he does for a living?"

"Does it really matter, Mom?" I asked.

"Yes. I want to know that he will be able to provide for you and—"

"Mom, we're not talking marriage or engagement here," I interrupted. "We're just dating."

"What type of work does he do?"

"Andre is a police detective."

"A what? You're dating a policeman? Nikki, what kind of life can a policeman's salary provide?"

"He's a *detective*, Mom, and I—"

"But he's still a policeman," she interrupted. "With all these shootings going on, he—"

"I have to go, Mom," I interrupted. "Tell Dad—"

"And he has to work odd hours, doesn't he? When will he have time for you?"

I sighed. "Tell Dad I love him. I'll talk with you soon. I love you, Mom."

"We love you, too, darling. Call me when you get back."

"Um, sure."

I knew she meant well, but that woman could be almost impossible at times. I shook my head and smiled. Well, at least this might keep her quiet about my love life.

I bit my lower lip.

No. She would still be searching for a doctor to "provide" for me.

CHAPTER 8

I was putting the finishing touches on my makeup when the doorbell rang. This time I had a pretty good idea who it was. I reached for Estée Lauder Pleasures, my favorite perfume, and dabbed a little behind my ears, on my neck, and across the tops of each of my breasts. I visualized Andre kissing each place I had dabbed. The thought of him turned me on. I winked at myself in the mirror before going to the door to let Andre in. I caught his gaze, and he caught mine. I was instantly mesmerized. He was one gorgeous hunk of man. He wore a cream-colored linen suit with a peach shirt and matching tie. He held a bouquet of colorful flowers in his hand.

"Baby, you look absolutely stunning," he said as he closed the distance between us.

He pulled me into him with his free hand, capturing my lips with his. He moaned as he deepened the kiss, exploring every inch of my mouth with his tongue while his hand caressed my butt. He slowly released his hold on me—both hand and lips. Taking a step back, he looked me up and down.

"You are one beautiful lady. I've never seen you with your hair up. It's stunning."

"Are you undressing me with your eyes?"

"If I say yes, will you hold yourself against me?"

I smiled. "Of course I will."

"Then I have to say ... no."

"No?"

"I undressed you with my eyes the second I came through the door."

I was at a loss for words. The magnetic power this man had over me was indescribable. I got such a charge from him. My brain turned to mush.

"Thank you," I murmured. "You look very handsome yourself."

He smiled brightly, handing me the flowers. "These are for you."

"Thanks. They're beautiful."

I walked into the kitchen to fill a vase with water for the flowers, still feeling weak in the knees from our kiss.

I turned to him. "I've been thinking about something. You said that your parents are celebrating fifteen years of marriage. I'm not trying to be nosy, but the numbers don't add up. Why is it only fifteen years that your parents have been married?" I couldn't believe I had blurted it out like that. I was starting to sound like my mother.

He studied me for a moment and frowned. "It's a bit of a story. Why don't I tell you in the car on the way over to my father's house?"

Father's house? This is getting more puzzling by the minute.

I retouched my makeup and applied fresh lipstick before we headed out the door.

"You look so sexy that I can't wait to get you back home," he said seductively, smacking me on my butt.

I can't wait either. I smiled brightly, thoughts of having sizzling hot sex with this gorgeous hunk running rampant through my head.

When we reached the front of my building, I saw a black limousine parked at the curb, the driver holding the door open. I was looking for Andre's Audi.

"Where did you park?" I asked with a puzzled look.

"I didn't drive my car. My father sent the limo for us."

"Huh?" I swallowed.

"He wants us to have a good time partying without having to worry about driving back. He insisted I take the limo." He grinned.

I entered the limousine. Andre climbed in

behind me, and the driver closed the door. Andre didn't give the driver instructions—he obviously knew our destination. With the push of a button, a glass partition slid into place between the driver and us, giving us privacy. Andre seemed pretty comfortable in the limo as if he had ridden in it on more than one occasion.

"Would you like something to drink?" He revealed a small bar area equipped with alcoholic beverages.

I shook my head. "Do you take the limo often?"

"No. Not really. Occasionally, my father insists on me using it, but I prefer driving my Audi." He smiled.

He took my hand in his, intertwined our fingers, and kissed the back of my hand. He leaned in closer and planted soft kisses down my neck, instantly moistening me, making me throb. "Why do you ask?"

"You don't seem like the limo type. I was just wondering."

He leaned back a bit and laughed. "So what type am I?"

"I don't know. I don't have a particular type in mind. I just never pictured you in a limo." *I must sound like an idiot. What the hell am I thinking?* I decided to change the subject before it got any worse and get to the bottom of this fifteen-year marriage thing. "I'm still curious to know about your parents' fifteen-year marriage."

"You're not going to let that go, are you?" He grinned. "I know it sounds strange ... Well, Monica is my father's second wife." His smile disappeared, and he sighed.

I squeezed his hand. "Andre, it's okay if you don't want to talk about it. You answered my question when you said she's your father's second wife." *Who am I kidding? I do want to know more, but I don't want to push him if he isn't ready.*

"It's okay, baby," he said. "I think it's time that I tell you more about me. I was barely out of my teens when my father married Monica. She's not much older than I am. I think the age difference bothers me more than it bothers the two of them."

"Wow!" I gasped. "How does your mom feel about your father marrying someone so much younger?"

"My mother's dead." He looked away, his head down.

"I'm so sorry, Andre ... I didn't mean—"

"Don't be sorry. You didn't know." He stroked my cheek softly. "Come closer."

He wrapped his arm around me tightly and gently rested his free hand on my thigh.

89

He cleared his throat. "When I was about fifteen, my mother was brutally raped and murdered. She had been missing for two days before the police found her body, which was covered in stab wounds, cigarette burns, and rope burns around her arms and legs."

The Vanessa Rojas case! God, that case must be really tough on him. I saw a tear in the corner of his eye and brushed it away with my thumb. "Andre, babe, you don't have to go on. I can see this is upsetting you. I don't want you to go through that pain just to explain something to me."

"It's okay. I want to tell you." He turned to me. "My dad didn't want to disrupt my school and soccer schedule, so he insisted I continue with my classes and practice those two days she was missing. There wasn't much anyone could do except wait to hear from the police. I had been dropped off at my house from practice one day by the mother of a teammate, and there was an unmarked police car in our driveway. I remember feeling nauseous when I saw it. I felt in the pit of my stomach that this wasn't good. I walked as slowly as I could to the front door, and I had second thoughts about going in. When I let myself into the house, I walked into the living room and immediately saw my father's face—saw the pain and anguish there. I had never seen him look so broken. My heart sank to my stomach. I knew that something horrible must have happened to my mother. My father stood and walked over to me and hugged me tightly. He began to break down, sobbing as he told me that the police had found my mother's body. I knew he wasn't lying, but I didn't want to believe him. I cried and shouted that it wasn't true, that it had to be a mistake. I wanted that policeman to leave. He was a reminder of a tragedy that I did not want to believe had happened." He took a deep breath and exhales.

Tears filled my eyes as I thought about the tragic loss of his mother and the horrific way she had died. I caressed his hand and kissed him softly on the lips. I didn't want to stop him from telling his story—it was therapeutic for him to let it out. I was so grateful that he felt comfortable enough with me to share it. In that moment, I discovered I had truly fallen in love with this man. My heart was breaking for him.

"The police never found my mother's murderer," he said.

"That's so sad."

"Yeah." He nodded. "There were a lot of leads but nothing leading to any arrests—all reasons why I am so determined to find Vanessa Rojas's killer."

"You will. I know it."

"I hope so."

"What made you want to be a detective?"

"My mother," he said. "She was a huge factor. I couldn't do anything to help her back then, and this is my way of honoring her."

"She would be so proud."

"I hope she would." He sighed. "She wouldn't be proud of my dad." He shook his head. "Monica is ... something else/off the chain/crazy as shit (something), yet somehow my dad loves her."

"You don't?"

"No. She tries to mother me sometimes."

"She's only a few years older, right?"

He nodded. "We have had some arguments, whoo! We barely get along now, but because of her, I have a stepsister, Katie. She's seven, and I adore her."

"Will she be at the party?"

"Sure," Andre said. "All of my crazy family will be there."

"They're not all crazy, right?"

"You'll see."

As we rode the rest of the way in a comfortable and peaceful silence, wrapped in each other's arms, my head resting on his chest, I wondered how crazy his family could get.

CHAPTER 9

We arrived at Andre's father's house, and my eyes grew wide with amazement. The limousine pulled into a large circular herringbone-patterned driveway, complete with a gurgling fountain. The grounds were beautifully manicured with an array of colorful flowers and shrubbery. The house was very large with a stucco and brick façade and stately architectural columns. As we entered the house through double doors, I heard the sound of people chatting, but I was more fascinated by my surroundings. The foyer was grand with an ornate tray ceiling from which hung an elegant crystal chandelier. A rich cherry wood table with Queen Anne legs topped with a huge crystal vase overflowing with an exotic flower arrangement held center stage. At either side of the foyer, dual staircases curved up to the second floor. Wall hangings of burgundy and cream and an array of interesting water color paintings adorned the fawn-colored walls. The flooring looked to be of the finest marble. The decorations were lavish and luxurious with the most exquisite detailing throughout. I turned to Andre, about to speak, when I saw amusement on his face. *Was I drooling?*

"Why are you looking at me like that?" I asked, feeling a wee bit annoyed.

"How am I looking at you?"

"Like you're amused."

"You look so ... I don't know if the word 'surprised' aptly describes your expression." He chuckled.

"I just didn't expect ... I'm amazed ... I mean . . ."

He put his arm around me. "My dad is a very wealthy man. This house is modest in comparison to what he can afford."

"But you're a cop. Uh ... I mean, there's nothing wrong with being a cop." *Mom's voice could pop up at the most unexpected times!*

"I love my job. I wouldn't trade it for anything. Yes, I come from a wealthy family, but I'm doing what I love."

"You really are full of surprises," I said gingerly.

He kissed my forehead, reached for my hand, and led the way into the large room across the foyer decorated lavishly with large wooden antique furniture, antique Persian rugs, and custom wall tapestry. A few people gathered there, drinking various cocktails, talking and laughing. Andre nodded to a few and stopped to introduce me to several groups as we made our way through a spacious sunroom, beautifully decorated with wicker furniture and exotic plants, that led to the back of the house. The landscaping there was even more breathtaking than that in the front. Swans roamed a small lake, and the lawn was dressed with colorful blooms, trees, statues and yet another fountain. Several long tables decorated with white tablecloths and chairs dressed in white cloth with large satin bows embellishing the back lined the lawn. Vases filled with beautiful white lilies adorned all the tables, which featured elegant china place settings. A few tables were positioned beneath white canopies. The whole scene looked as if it had been taken from a page in a decorating magazine.

My jaw dropped as I took in the opulence, but I managed to draw it back up as a couple approached us. I could tell as they got closer that the man was Andre's father because Andre was his spitting image. The woman much younger than the man—tall, thin, and attractive. She had very long beautiful, silky, black hair and green eyes.

The man grabbed Andre and gave him a tight hug. "Son!" He smiled widely at me.

"Hi, Dad!" Andre grinned at his father. I could see the love between them. To Monica, Andre offered a slight smile. He turned to me and placed his arm around my waist. "This is Nicole."

"Nice to meet you." I extended my hand to Andre's father.

He stared at me intensely for a few seconds. "Robert." He ignored my hand and pulled me toward him, gave me a hug, and kissed my cheek. I smiled and shifted on my feet. I'm normally not shy, but his hug caught me off guard, and I didn't know how to react.

Monica extended her hand, and I shook it, smiling. "Nice to meet you, Monica."

I could feel the tension between Andre and her. I wondered if it was real or imagined—or some women's intuition thing I had picked up during our conversation in the car. As that thought danced in my head, an adorable little girl appeared. She ran up to Andre, and he scooped her up and twirled her around as she squealed with glee. "Andre, Andre! You're here!"

He planted noisy kisses on her cheek. "Hello, princess!" he said cheerfully and carefully placed her back on her feet.

"Katie, this is Nicole," he said, pulling me in closer to him.

"Hi, Katie." I smiled brightly.

"Hi, are you Andre's girlfriend?" she asked as she twirled strands of her hair around her finger.

"Katie!" her dad said with a look of embarrassment.

I was also embarrassed by the question and didn't quite know how to answer it. Andre and I had never discussed labels, although our friends all assumed we were a couple.

"Yes, she is," Andre interrupted, and he kissed my lips.

My heart skipped a beat. *Does this mean that we are now officially a couple?*

"Well, she's beautiful, you know," Katie said matter-of-factly, and I blushed.

As I looked around, I noticed that more people were starting to arrive. I also noticed musicians were setting up their equipment. Robert walked over to a microphone that had already been set up. He requested everyone to be seated. We all crossed the lawn to our respective seats. Andre held Katie's hand in one of his, and he kept his arm around my waist. We took our seats.

As Robert continued speaking about his years of marriage to Monica, I took a moment to observe the people sitting around us. I caught an attractive woman at a table across from us gazing directly at

Andre. When I looked at him, he seemed to have become aware of her attention as well, but I couldn't read his expression, which made me feel a bit uneasy. While everyone around us raised their glasses to toast Robert and Monica, I sat motionless, so focused on the exchange between Andre and the mystery woman that I didn't raise my glass. When I snapped out of it, I picked up my glass and raised it along with the others. The band began to play music shortly after Robert had finished his speech. Andre and the mystery woman continued to exchange gazes. This reminded me of the funny looks that my so-called best friend, Gail, and that son of a bitch Michael used to give each other. I stood without saying anything to him and walked toward the entrance to the house. I heard him calling me, but I didn't stop. I had to get out of there. I didn't know where I was going, but I needed to get as far away as possible. I had reached the foyer area with the dual staircases when I felt a tug on my arm. Startled, I turned around. It was Andre. He frowned.

"Nicole, what's wrong? Why did you leave? Where are you going?"

"Really?" I said, tears forming in my eyes.

"I don't understand. What upset you, babe? Did someone say something or do something?"

"Stop it, Andre! What kind of fool do you take me for?" I used my hand to release his grip.

I pulled out my cell phone to call a taxi to take me home. *Sheesh! I don't have a number for a taxi. Fuck!* I decided to call one of the girls and have them look up a taxi number for me.

"Nicole, talk to me, baby! Please! I don't think you're a fool. What are you talking about?" He reached out to touch me, but I put my hand up, motioning for him to back off.

"Listen, I want to go home now. Can you please call me a taxi?"

"You're not going anywhere until you tell me what's going on." He reached out for me again, refusing my resistance. "Come with me to the library. Let's talk in private."

I hadn't noticed until now that a man and woman who had entered the room near the foyer were now staring in our direction. I didn't want to make a spectacle of myself, so I decided to take Andre up on his offer for privacy.

The library was a large, brightly lit room with a wooden ledge that bordered the entire room. Each wall contained shelves of books across the entire top of the ledge and beneath it. The only break in the continuum of bookshelves was a section of large windows extending above and below the ledge, giving the appearance of floor-to-ceiling windows. The room was colorful for a library—decorated with red leather sofas and chairs, glass-top tables with brass legs, and a beautiful oriental rug overlaying the polished cherry wood floor. A ladder was positioned in front of one of the corner bookshelves. I was so taken in by my surroundings that I'd almost forgotten why we were here.

"Babe, have a seat and tell me what's wrong," he said, motioning toward one of the sofas.

I cut my eyes at him sharply, ignoring the gesture. Entering the library with its beauty and warmth seemed to have shifted my mood. I felt more settled. I didn't feel as vulnerable as I had previously.

Andre took my hand and led me to one of the sofas, and this time I didn't resist. I sat on its soft leather cushion, looked down at the bracelet I wore on my wrist, and began fumbling with the charm. "Who is she?" I asked, not sure whether I actually wanted to hear his response.

"Who are you talking about?" he asked.

I stared at him blankly. Surely he must know who I meant. I wondered for a moment if he was being arrogant or if I was silly for asking.

"The woman sitting across from us," I retorted. "I saw you looking at her."

"Are you serious, Nicole? That's what this is

about?" He sighed and ran his fingers through his hair.

I had noticed that he did that when he became frustrated. I felt my face start to flush. I had never been the jealous type. *Is it jealously that I'm feeling?* Beyond my control, a teardrop rolled down my cheek, and he gently wiped it away.

"Come here, baby," he said so sweetly. "I promised you that I would never hurt you, and I intend to keep that promise." He patted his lap, motioning for me to sit there, embracing me once I slid into place.

"The woman you're speaking of is an ex-girlfriend whom I want nothing to do with."

I raised up from his lap, but he held me tighter so that I couldn't leave.

"Nicole, listen to me. You wanted to know who she is, so hear me out."

"I can't believe you'd invite me to an affair knowing that your ex-girlfriend would be attending. What kind of sick game are you playing?" Tears swelled in my eyes.

"I had no idea she'd be here. When you saw me looking at her, I was attempting to manipulate her into leaving. In fact, I had planned on going over to her to tell her to leave." He frowned.

"Why is she here? I don't understand." I made another unsuccessful attempt to escape his lap.

He rolled his eyes and looked up into the air. "Because she's a friend of Monica's. She must have invited her. I will get to the bottom of this with her and my father, although I'm sure that my father was not aware of it. Nicole, honey, I swear to you on my mother's grave, she means nothing at all to me. We broke up a few years ago. She lied to me about something very important, and I have never forgiven her for that, besides the fact that she is a gold digger." He stroked my face softly with his finger and wipes away more teardrops. "You have nothing to worry about, baby. You are the only woman who has my interest."

He leaned closer and took full possession of my lips and mouth. He slid his hand up my dress, caressed my thighs slowly in circular motions until he reached my thong. He gently pulled my thong to one side and teased my pearl relentlessly, awakening my desire to be taken right there. I moaned softly with each stroke. He pushed one finger into my moistened valley, and I began to move my hips as he slowly pulled it out again then pushed two fingers in deeply which made my body quiver with ecstasy as I moaned. I came to my senses enough to realize we were in his father's library, and anyone could enter at any moment.

"Andre, someone might come in," I whispered.

"Which makes it all the more exciting, wouldn't you say?" He grinned mischievously.

I have to admit, he had a point there. I was intrigued.

"Nicole, do you trust me?" He stared into my eyes.

He is so damn hot. I'm not sure of how to respond. I bit my lip. "How do you mean?" *Where is he going with this?* My stomach was turning flips. I had a feeling this trust thing had nothing to do with the ex-girlfriend, but his cell phone rang as he was about to respond.

"Detective Moore." He frowned. "Fuck!" He stood and began pacing the floor, running his hand through his beautiful, black hair. "I'm on my way. It'll take some time to get there—I'm on Long Island. Call me with any updates." He turned to me. "Unfortunately, we have to leave now. Something's come up at work that needs my attention."

He searched his phone and tapped in a number. "Harold, bring the car around."

I touched his arm gently. "Andre, are you okay?" I didn't know what else to say. The color seemed to have drained from his face. Whatever that phone call had been about, it wasn't good.

"I'm fine, let's go."

I followed him as he raced out of the library and through the foyer. A few people gathered there chatted as we rushed past them and out the front door. Our driver, Harold, stood next to the black stretch limo, the door held open for us to enter. He waited until we were secured inside the car and then closed the door behind us.

"Harold, we're taking Ms. Watkins home first," Andre instructed.

"Andre, whatever's going on with your job really seems to be upsetting you. Is it something you can talk about?" I gently caressed his hand.

"Nicole, you know I can't discuss this with you," he said as he scrolled through his iPhone with his index finger.

"Seriously, Andre? Do you think I'd leak something to the public without your authorization? I was asking as a concerned friend, off the record."

"Even so, I can't discuss it ... yet." He looked up from his iPhone. "I need more information."

His phone rang again. I judged from the conversation that it was the same person who had called previously. His face became even more intense. I wondered what was getting Detective

Andre so upset. *Detective*. I seemed to revert to his official title when he became immersed in business. By the time he ended the phone call, we had pulled up to my apartment building.

"Baby, I'm sorry I was on the phone so long. I wouldn't have taken the call if it hadn't been urgent."

I studied him for a moment. "You're a homicide detective. There's no need to apologize when you get a call regarding your work." *That's it! The call must have something to do with a murder!* That had to be the reason he had to rush off to work.

Harold came around and opened the limo door. Darkness had fallen and, although it was a summer night, a chill ran through my body. Andre, so in tune with my body, held me close as we walked down the sidewalk. I always felt so safe and protected when I was with him. We walked in silence. Although I desperately wanted to question him further—my reporter instincts kicking in—I chose to let it go. I didn't want to add to the heavy load that already seemed to be weighing on him. Peeking out of the window as he left, I watched as he got back into the car and it rolled out of view. I stood there for a moment, pondering the events of the day and what Andre would have to face once he arrived at his destination.

Hmm. Maybe when he's done with that police business, he will come back and finish what he started in the library ...

CHAPTER 10

Sunday seemed to have flown by. I had made no plans because Andre and I were going to spend the day together, but that fell through when he called to tell me he had to work. He apologized, said he had an important case and couldn't get away, and promised to make it up to me. I thought it probably had to do with the calls he received yesterday. He still hadn't shared any information about them with me.

Both Janice and Joann were unavailable, too. Janice was visiting her sister in New Jersey, and Joann was visiting a friend in Brooklyn, so I decided to do some late spring cleaning in July. I cleaned out closets, bagging clothes, shoes, and purses for charity. I scrubbed the kitchen cabinets inside and out, washed windows, polished furniture, mopped floors, and vacuumed carpets. All that housecleaning was exhausting. *I am going to check into housecleaning services for my next big cleaning job.* Once the marathon cleaning session was finished,

I took a long shower, ate a turkey sandwich, and fell quickly to sleep while watching a *Sex in the City* episode.

******

I was awakened by the sound of my cell phone ringing. The clock on my nightstand read four a.m. I wondered who would be calling me at this ungodly hour. I didn't recognize the number on my phone and normally wouldn't have answered an unfamiliar number, but something bothered me about this call. Still half-asleep, I answered the phone.

To my surprise, it was Andre. "I'm sorry to wake you, my angel."

Wow! He called me angel—and I love it! I lay grinning in the dark for a few seconds before regaining my composure. "Andre! Are you okay? What number are you calling from?"

"I'm fine. I'm using my work phone because my cell needs charging. Listen, how soon can you get into the city?" He seemed to be asking with a sense of urgency.

"I don't know. Maybe about an hour. Why? What's going on?"

"Nicole, what I'm about to tell you is off the record until you get here. Understand?" He sounded serious.

"Okay." I rolled my eyes, frustrated that he still didn't get that I wouldn't report anything without his permission.

"There's been another murder." His voice lowered. "I want you to have the exclusive."

I knew it! That explained last night's phone call. "Was it like Vanessa Rojas?"

"You know I can't talk about that over the phone. What station do you come out of? I can pick you up in about an hour."

"I'll be taking the E train, so I'll be at the Lexington Avenue and Fifty-third Street station."

"I'll be there by the time you are. And Nicole?"

"Yes?"

"Please be careful," he said.

"I will. See you soon."

I sprang from my bed. My sudden move frightened Freddie, who leaped from the bed and skedaddled out of the room. I believed Freddie thought I was a madwoman at times. I took a quick shower, pulled my damp hair up in a ponytail, and dressed in a hurry. After brushing a little mascara onto my eyelashes, I dashed out the door in record time at around 4:30 a.m.

******

Only a handful of people waited for the subway when I arrived at the station. I made it onto the platform just as the E train pulled in. It was odd boarding a half-empty train that would normally be packed with standing room only—correction, squeezing room only. I sat in one of the many empty seats available and took my compact mirror from my purse to see if I looked decent since I had had no time to put on my usual makeup except for the mascara. Assessing my appearance, I thought a little lipstick would do the trick. I reached into my purse again and—lucky me—found a lipstick buried under all the junk I carried around. *I need to clean out this purse.*

As I applied the lipstick as best I could with the train both shaking and coming to abrupt halts, I felt as if I was being watched. I glanced up from the mirror and saw a shabby-looking man sitting in the seat directly across from me, grinning at me with his hand down inside his pants, rubbing his penis. *Ugh! Really?* Prior to living in New York, such an act would have really paralyzed me with fright, but since moving here, I had already seen just about it all. The train was about to pull into the station. When it stopped and the doors opened, I exited that subway car and hurried into another before the doors closed. I wasn't going to spend the rest of my train ride with that pervert. More people populated the next car, but I was still able to get a seat.

The train pulled into the Lexington Avenue and 53rd Street station. When I came up to street level, Andre was standing there waiting for me, looking so deliciously hot. I couldn't believe he was *my* gorgeous hunk of man. He smiled at me as soon as our eyes met. As I got closer, I could tell he hadn't had much sleep—if any—because of the dark circles under his eyes, but it didn't diminish his good looks one iota. He embraced me and kissed me on the lips.

"Good morning, angel."

Hmmm, I could get used to this.

He took my hand and led me to a double-parked, unmarked police car. He held the passenger door open for me, and I slid in. It was a cool summer morning with a slight breeze, but the forecast called for a humid day. When Andre got into the driver's seat, he handed me breakfast—a cup of coffee and a brown paper bag holding a bagel with cream cheese.

"The least I could do since I got you out of bed so early," he grinned.

My heart swelled. It was the little things he did that brought me such joy. I didn't usually eat this early in the morning, but I had a feeling it was going to be a long one, and I probably wouldn't have any time to grab a bite to eat later. Besides, Andre had gone out of his way to make sure I had something to eat.

"Thank you, very sweet of you," I said, giving him my version of the Mona Lisa smile.

He smiled back and then leaned in and kissed me softly. He stared at me intensely, his face still close to mine. "I love you."

Holy Sweet Jesus! Did he just say what I think he said? My heart skipped three—or ten!—beats while my stomach did several somersaults. I froze. *Really, Nikki? Say something!* my inner self kept nudging. I swallowed, my throat dry. "Um, wow, that was—"

We were rudely interrupted by a man knocking on the window of the car.

"Hey, move it, buddy! I'm trying to get into that parking spot!" He pointed to a spot near us which had become vacant.

Frowning, Andre turned toward his window and flashed his police badge. "Back off."

The man didn't apologize. He rolled his eyes and walked back to his car.

Andre turned to me and shook his head, muttering, "Some nerve," as he started the car engine and drove off.

I was still spending time in seventh heaven over his confession of love for me. I took a sip of coffee to wet my dry throat. "Would it be okay for me to call my boss to let him know I'm working on a story? I'm due at work in a couple of hours, and I'd like him to know I might not be there on time."

He took a moment to answer. "Don't go into any detail with him."

"Andre, I don't have any details to give him! But he'll want to have some idea what it's about." I waited impatiently for his reply.

"I don't like it, but all right. Just tell him I'm giving you an exclusive on a murder case, but you don't have the details yet, and *nothing* is to go to print until you get back to your office."

"I don't believe I would have said anything different," I smirked.

He glanced at me, grimacing. "Don't get cute with me."

I turned my head toward the window, a stupid grin on my face. He was so hot when he got serious. I reached into my purse and took out my cell phone to call Mr. Blackman.

"Look, if you're going to be late, just say so," Mr. Blackman said. "You don't have to—"

"I'm riding with a detective, Mr. Blackman," I interrupted. "I'm on the case." I always wanted to say that.

"Which case?"

"I can't say..."

"It's the Rojas case, isn't it?"

"I can't say, Mr. Blackman…"

He wasn't thrilled about me calling him so early in the morning, but he was pleased to hear I was working on another exclusive story with the police department. After my story on the Vanessa Rojas case, sales of the newspaper had risen sharply.

The neighborhood we were driving through looked familiar. "Andre, where are we going? Isn't this where you brought me to show me where Vanessa Rojas was murdered? What's it called again? The Lincoln Houses?"

His expression became grim. "Yes. This is where we were. The Rojas live three buildings away from where we're going."

We pulled up in front of one of the run-down buildings. He parked the car, turned the engine off, and faced me. "I want to brief you on the case before we get out of the car." He shifted straight into detective mode.

I reached down into my briefcase on the floor of the car—I had brought it along since I planned to go straight to work from my meeting with Andre—and pulled out my pad to take notes. When I looked up, Andre had the same glum expression on his face he had when I interviewed him about the other case.

"Andre, what is it?" I asked.

"Well, as I already mentioned on the phone, it's another murder case," he muttered.

"Duh, I already knew that." *He's really testing my nerves right now.* "Detective, get to the point."

He studied me for a moment with what seemed to be a hint of irritation. "I thought we were long past 'detective'."

"We were until you settled back into that role. The way you're behaving now, for instance."

"I'm trying to get my thoughts together—what you need to know *on* the record and what I'm willing to tell you *off*."

"All right, why don't we begin with on the record?"

"The case seems to have the same M.O. Umm ... that is, *modus operandi*."

"Yes, I know what M.O. means."

"The victim is another sixteen-year-old girl, also brutally raped and murdered. She also lived here in the Lincoln Houses. Just like Vanessa did." He frowned and reached over to grab a file from the back seat of the car. He looked at me. "I have pictures from the scene. This time I'm asking you if you want to see them before I show them to you."

The pictures of the crime scene from Vanessa Rojas' murder were etched in my head—I didn't think I would ever be able to get rid of the images.

My stomach began to knot as my brain spit out flashbacks of the previous horror. *Come on, Nikki, you can do this!* "Yes, let me take a look." My lips formed the words bravely as my eyes braced for what I was about to see.

"Before I show you, I want to make you aware that this assault took place on the rooftop of the victim's apartment building."

"Jesus!" I tried to calm myself before reaching for the pictures. Taking a deep breath, I brought the photos into my view. "For the love of God!" I exclaimed.

My heart dove to my stomach. The pictures revealed a young African American girl. She lay naked on the concrete floor of a rooftop, her clothing crumpled in a pile a few feet away. Just like Vanessa Rojas, she had multiple stab wounds to her body. Her body was bruised and had what appeared to be cigarette burns covering it. Both of her eyes were blackened. Blood had pooled around her body and stained gravel on the rooftop. I closed my eyes for a moment, feeling queasiness rush over me. I sighed and handed the pictures back to Andre. "What a sick son of a bitch!"

"How are you?" Andre asked.

"I'm fine. I just don't understand what could

make a person so evil. How could anyone do something so horrific?"

He took my hand and caressed it gently. "He's a psychopath, and unless you're an expert in knowing the mindset of a psychopath, you'll never understand. I don't think that even the experts really know what makes them tick."

"I guess you're right," I muttered, still feeling a bit sick to my stomach. But at least I didn't come close to fainting this time. "What's the name of the girl in the pictures?"

"Andrea Brown." He tucked the pictures back into the folder. "Her mother called the precinct because she had been missing for two days."

"Did the police find her body on the rooftop?"

"Yes, umm ... no. Actually, a call came in from a maintenance man. They were doing some work on the rooftop when one of them discovered the body and called the police."

"Why did the mother wait two days to call the police? Two days? What kind of mother is that?"

Andre got out of the car and came around to my side to open the door. Humidity was beginning to filter into what began as a cool summer morning. We entered the building, whose lobby smelled like a mixture of urine, cigarettes, and sewage, and waited for the elevator. A man wearing blue jeans and a

Knicks jersey came from the stairway, scowling as he walked past us and out the door.

"We're taking the elevator to the top floor and then the stairway to the rooftop. Are you going to be okay with this?"

I nodded.

The door to the elevator opened, and a woman dressed in a business suit holding a briefcase stood there. "Excuse me," she said as she left the elevator and pushed past us. She was wearing perfume with a strong fragrance. The smell lingered in the air even after she walked past.

When the elevator reached the top floor, we exited and then climbed a staircase leading up to the roof. Strips of yellow crime scene tape dangled from the frame of the door that led out onto the rooftop. Andre guided me over to the spot where the young girl's body had been found.

I turned to face him. "Where's the chalk outline of the body? There's nothing to indicate a body was here besides remnants of dried blood."

"You can't be serious."

"I am serious. Isn't that how it's done?"

"You watch way too many old TV shows. That's no longer procedure in homicide cases. It used to be done temporarily to preserve evidence but was found to actually contaminate it, so we stopped the practice. It also allowed the press to get pictures of the crime scene without worrying about the gruesomeness of a dead body. Anyway, we have long since replaced the chalk with removable flags."

"Oh ... I see."

I walked around the bloodstained area, trying not to think of the horror that young girl must have gone through. I looked up and gazed around at the surrounding buildings, not sure exactly what I was looking for. I'm no investigator, and I'm sure the police had combed the entire rooftop looking for evidence that may have been left behind.

"Did the assault take place during the daytime?"

"Yes. The medical examiner's report states the time of death as sometime during the afternoon hours."

"Was it also the same for Vanessa Rojas? Did her murder also take place during the day?"

"Yes."

"So why is it that a strange man was not seen with either of the victims?" I asked, trying to piece together the commonalities of the two murders. "Surely, someone must have seen him with the girls at some point."

"First of all, don't get ahead of yourself playing detective. Although it seems to be the same M.O., it could very well be two different people. We're investigating all possibilities."

"I'm just doing my job, Andre. I don't want to step on anybody's toes, but I need as much information as I can get to write an authentic article." *Men and their egos.* "In the car, you said something to me about how you were unsure if you were willing to tell me something off the record. What might that be? Do the police have any leads?"

He studied me for a moment. "We are following several leads. This may not sound like much, but it's something we don't want to see in the papers until we've had more time to investigate." He squinted. "It seems that both girls attended the same high school and were in the same grade."

"Why would the police not want the press to know that? Anyone could check that out with one call to the school."

"It took more than one call, believe me, because neither girl attended school all that regularly," Andre said. "And we don't want the press to know because we don't want to alarm parents if it's just a coincidence—which it very well may be."

We spent a few minutes more going over the crime scene, and I jotted down some notes:

Body facing east, 63 windows facing the roof,

secluded, sound doesn't travel, maybe someone heard something not sure what it was, door to roof unlocked, open to anyone...empty wine bottles, cigarette butts

I looked up to see Andre yawn.

"Tired?"

"Yeah, it's been a long night and day."

"Maybe it's time that you get home and get some rest." I shoved my notepad into my bag.

He closed the distance between us.

"I will after I get you back to work." He lowered his lips onto mine and kissed me softly.

I shuddered.

"You okay?"

"It's just so ... weird to have you kiss me while I'm here ... where a girl died."

"Sorry."

"It's okay," I said. "I really needed that kiss."

CHAPTER 11

It felt great to be working on another story that showcased my skills as a journalist. Unfortunately, it was another tragic story. I had gone over and over the similarities of the two murders and felt it was the same person who had raped and murdered both of these girls. Why was he choosing girls of the same age who lived in the same housing complex? Could the murderer be someone who also lived in the same place? Could it be someone that they had known—someone who wasn't a stranger to them? So many questions and thoughts whirled around my mind.

I also thought about Andre and how he had to relive—for the second time—a tragedy similar to his own mother's. I know this had to be taking a toll on him, but he was determined to solve both cases. I hoped he didn't let them consume him to the point where he lost himself and became bitter.

I was lost in thought and didn't notice Blackman

standing beside my desk with a stupid grin on his face. Grinning, by the way, was a rarity for him.

"Ms. Watkins, I pulled some strings to get you that first assignment on the rape/murder case, but tell me something ... Why were you contacted by the police for this recent case?" He looked at me, his bushy eyebrows doing pushups.

It was no secret that Andre and I were dating, but I didn't think it appropriate—or professional, for that matter—to discuss my personal life with my boss. I was about to answer when my desk phone rang, and I picked it up. The caller was Blackman's secretary.

"Mr. Blackman, it's Pam. She says you have an urgent phone call."

"We'll finish this conversation another time," he said as he turned and walked past the row of cubicles toward his office.

I was relieved not to have had to go into detail about how I was chosen for the exclusive on this story. Eventually, I'd have to do some explaining, but at least it wouldn't be today.

I was in the middle of returning phone calls, answering emails, and doing some research for other news articles when Janice rolled her chair into my cubicle, flashing a wide smile.

"Hey, Nikki. How'd it go with the anniversary celebration Saturday?"

I chuckled. "It was definitely eventful."

"Why? What happened?"

"I'm going to have to save that story for when I can talk to you and Joann together. Are we still on for dinner?"

"Of course we are. I can't wait to hear what happened!"

"Great! Let's wrap things up here and be on our way."

******

Janice and I met Joann at one of our favorite Italian restaurants, Malatesta Trattoria, in the West Village. It was a casual restaurant—small but cozy and inexpensive. I loved their homemade pasta and grilled calamari, a great alternative to the fried kind. It had a nice charred taste but was still chewy and juicy. We were seated right away—a good thing because I was famished. Joann seemed as eager as Janice to learn about my weekend.

"So how did the party go?" With her elbows on the table, cupping her face with both her hands, Joann was all ears.

I looked up from skimming the menu to find them both staring at me expectantly, beaming. "As I mentioned to Janice earlier, it was eventful," I said, smiling slyly.

"You mean you told Janice about it already?" Joann pouted.

"Calm yourself down. I told Janice that I would tell the two of you together." I shook my head. "Well, his folks seem pretty nice, although his *very* young, beautiful stepmother ... hmm ... she's a bit too young to be referred to as his stepmother. Well, anyway, I don't think she cares for me much."

Simultaneously, they both asked, "Why?" and laughed out loud.

I smiled at their responses. Frankly, I didn't know the answer to that. I hadn't figured it out yet myself. "It's just a feeling I got when Andre introduced us. His father and little sister were both very receptive and quite pleasant, but she was kind of cold and indifferent. By the way, Andre looks very much like his father."

"Then his father must be hot, too!" Janice blurted and then blushed. "You know what I mean. Not that I'm checking out your man or anything, but he *is* a hottie."

"Yes, he is," I marveled while flashing back to his naked, muscular body. "Okay, getting back to what I was saying. The house was huge, beautiful, and very elegantly decorated. They actually have a lake in the back of the house." I shook my head. "And everything was going well until I caught Andre in a stare down with an ex-girlfriend."

Their jaws dropped. Janice was too stunned to respond while Joann sputtered, "Shut the front door!"

Janice recovered quickly, asking, "Why was his ex-girlfriend even there?"

The waitress brought our drinks to the table and set them down in front of us. She asked if we were ready to order. We all ordered salads with three different entrees to share so that we had a variety of food to choose from. Janice and Joann returned their attention to me as soon as the waitress stepped away.

"Well?" Janice asked, her feet tap-dancing under the table.

I took a slow sip from my glass of wine, and my friends grimaced. I did it only to wet my throat, but it was fun to watch them ooze with anticipation. I set the glass back down and cleared my throat. "He seems to think that his father's wife invited her because they're friends."

"This just keeps getting better." Janice snorted.

"Nikki, I'm surprised that Andre put you in such an awkward position," Joann said. "Having to be at a party with an ex-girlfriend *and* watching him stare at the woman right in front of you. Shame on him!"

I held my hands up in the air for a timeout. "Hold on a minute. It wasn't like that at all. Initially, that was what I thought, too. In fact, Andre and I got into a fight over it—or shall I say, he had some serious explaining to do. Turns out he and his dad had no idea the woman was invited, and he was trying to intimidate her into leaving with the stare down."

"How was staring at her going to get her to leave?" Janice asked.

"I asked the same thing. He said he'd planned to approach her to ask her to leave, but he didn't get a chance because I decided that *I* was going to leave. He ended up going after me."

The waitress was back at our table with our meals—the food looked and smelled delicious. I continued to tell the girls about my time at Andre's father's house in between bites of food, skipping the part about our little love-fest in the library, and Janice and Joann filled me in on their weekends. Janice's older sister and her husband were expecting another baby in the fall. She seemed quite cheerful about becoming an aunt again. Joann's friend in Brooklyn had become engaged to her long-term boyfriend and was planning a wedding next spring. Joann had been asked to be a part of the wedding party, and she was thrilled about it.

The conversation changed to the topic of the

most recent murder at the Lincoln Houses. Janice had some inside knowledge about the most recent murder because she worked with me at the newspaper. Joann was surprised that the killer had struck again in the same location. Unlike me, Janice wasn't convinced that it was the same person. She thought it could be a copycat. Without giving away any information Andre had given me off the record about the girls attending the same high school, I argued that there were too many similarities for it not to be the same person.

Joann nodded. "Has to be."

"Ladies, this is totally off topic, but here's one other thing that I'd almost forgotten to mention," I said cheerfully.

They both looked at me expectantly, waiting for me to continue.

"On second thought, maybe I shouldn't tell you ladies this," I teased. "Yep, I think I'll just keep this to myself."

"Oh no you don't," Joann growled softly.

"Okay, but don't make more out of it than what it is. I know how you two can—"

"Just tell us already," Janice interrupted.

"Andre told me that he loves me," I said, grinning from ear to ear. *I don't dare mention that I was an idiot and didn't say it back.*

Joann, who was sitting right next to me, leaned over and hugged me tightly. "Aww, that's so sweet. I'm very happy for you, honey."

Janice rose from her chair and reached over to give me a high five, almost knocking over her drink. "It's about time he told you what we already knew."

"So...is your man coming over tonight?" Joann asked.

"No, he's tired."

Joann suggested a toast. Each of us raised our glasses and said, "To love." It was so weird how we sometimes said the same thing simultaneously—that's how in tune we were within our friendship circle.

Yes, to love.

And finding a killer.

CHAPTER 12

The aroma of fresh coffee brewing awakened me from my sleep.

I smiled as I stretched my arm out to touch Andre before opening my eyes. The spot in the bed next to me where he had fallen asleep last night was empty. I smiled because that told me that the delicious fragrance was coming from his kitchen. Andre was up making breakfast. Now fully awake, I also smelled bacon cooking. My stomach growled in delight.

I lay in bed a few moments longer, allowing memories of an incredible night of lovemaking to float through my head. I lost count of the number of times we indulged. After a fun night out on the town, Andre drew a bath for me, filling the tub with bubbles. He sat on the edge of the tub, watching me intently as I undressed before him, removing one piece of clothing at a time in a slow, seductive manner. He stood up and reached for my hand, stopping me when my panties were the only piece of clothing left to be removed. He wanted to "do the honors," as he put it. He kissed me softly on the lips then deepened the kiss, giving me his tongue, which I greedily took in. He ended the kiss and kneeled in front of me. My stomach did cartwheels as he used both hands to slowly slide my panties down my hips. He was so close that I could feel his breaths tickling my pubic area, making my heartbeat quicken. He pulled my panties down further until they were past my knees. I bit my lip in anticipation. In a hoarse whisper, he instructed me to step out of them, and he then parted my legs with his hand and kissed my happy button. I pressed one hand against the wall to steady myself because my legs felt weak. He trailed kisses down my inner thigh, returning between my legs and nuzzling there for a moment and taking in my womanly scent. He looked up at me with those beautiful hazel eyes and whispered, "I want to taste you."

I became so heated with desire that it took everything in me to keep still. He gently teased my clit with his fingers and his tongue, sending me into a whirlwind of pleasure as my body quivered. He blew puffs of air onto my clit then dipped his tongue inside me, licking in circular motions. I moaned, my eyes closed in ecstasy. I felt my legs start to tremble.

I continued to hold the wall with one hand and his head with the other as he devoured me. He didn't let up. It was mind-blowing, electrifying, and exquisite. My breathing was out of control. I cried out as I exploded with an orgasm lasting longer than any I had ever experienced. It left me weak in the knees. Andre held me to keep me from falling.

"You all right?" he asked.

I nodded, speechless.

"Are you ready for your bath?" he asked.

I nodded. "I'm already, um, wet, though."

Andre smiled. "Yes you are."

He helped me into the tub, and as I submerged into the bubbly rose-scented water, it felt warm and comforting against my skin. Andre reached for the bath sponge and gently bathed my body, using slow gentle strokes across my skin. He helped me to a standing position and used a soft washcloth to caress my happy button, moving the cloth slowly in and out, igniting another orgasm.

He lifted the lever to drain the water from the tub. As the water drained, he began to undress, instructing me to remain standing there. As I watched him remove his clothing and gazed upon his naked body—tall, lean, muscular, well-endowed—desire began to blossom inside me. He stepped into the tub along with me and turned on the shower. He pulled me closer to him, directly under the flow of the water, and he bent to kiss me—not soft this time, but hard and deliberate and filled with passion.

He whispered in my ear, "Now it's your turn to bathe me."

I reached for the body wash, poured a little in my hand, and rubbed both hands together to create a rich lather. He closed his eyes as I moved my lathered hands slowly and gently across his magnificent chest and down the core of his body. He was fully erect. My heart raced, and I felt myself become moist and ready for him. I had never given a man head—not even my ex-husband—but I was overcome with the desire to please Andre in that way. I was turned on by the very thought of it.

Andre opened his eyes as if sensing what I was thinking. I smiled at him and took him in my hand, tightening my fingers while stroking up and down his erect member. It seemed to have grown even harder and thicker in my hand. He began moving his hips in response. Kneeling, I teased the tip with my tongue, flicking and twirling down his length before closing my lips around him. His breathing increased, and his hand gripped my hair gently. I began to take him deeper, sucking harder while caressing his testicles. He groaned louder. I could see the pleasure on his face—his mouth open, and his tongue licking his delicious lips.

"Baby, I'm going to cum now."

He tried to gently nudge my head so that he wouldn't cum into my mouth, but I refused to move. I wanted to taste him as he had tasted me. He thrust his hips harder as his hand gripped my hair tighter. He let out a guttural sound as a salty liquid trickled down my throat, initially causing me to gag a little.

He pulled me up into his arms and trailed soft kisses down my neck then gazed into my eyes and said, "I love you, baby. You mean so much to me. I think I've loved you from the moment that we met."

This time I didn't need a nudge from my inner self. I looked him in the eyes and said, "I love you, too."

I cupped shower water with my hand and rinsed my mouth, and then he kissed my lips softly and then ran his tongue across my lip as I parted my mouth for its entry. We kissed long and passionately. Breaking the kiss, he put his mouth to my nipple and nibbled it, twirling his tongue around and teasing it until I was on fire with desire. I moaned softly. He let go and positioned himself behind me. While he kissed the back of my neck, he guided my outstretched arms to the shower wall. He parted my legs gently with one of his legs and whispered in my ear, "Bend over—I want to take you from behind."

He reached around to the front of me, gently and slowly caressing my happy button while kissing the nape of my neck. I could feel his hardness pressing into my butt. My breathing increased. He gently entered me, deeper and deeper inside. I moaned. His thrusts began deliberately but increased in rhythm. Without warning, he spanked me across my butt several times while inside me. The sting of his hands against my delicate skin felt exhilarating. My body quivered with both pain and pleasure. He held me tighter as he pumped faster and harder.

"Baby, I want you *so* much. This feels *so* good."

My body trembled, and I moaned loudly as I exploded around him. He thrust even harder and groaned loudly as he poured himself into me.

"Um, baby, I think we need another bath/shower …"

Andre entered the room with a tray of breakfast food.

"Good morning, angel. I hope you're hungry." He flashed those pearly whites.

I sat up in bed and brushed away a few strands of hair that had fallen against my face. He stood before me, bare-chested and wearing only pajama bottoms. *Wow, he is just too hot* I thought as he set the tray across my lap and kissed me on the forehead. "Mmm ... I'm famished," I responded.

Bacon, eggs, buttered toast, orange juice, coffee, and a small bowl of fruit. But there was only one plate of food.

"You're not going to eat anything?" I asked, looking down at the food on the plate. "I can't eat all of this. It's too much! Have some with me."

"I'm not hungry. I have a confession to make—I had some cereal and toast earlier." He grinned sheepishly. "I got up really early because I couldn't sleep, and you were sleeping so peacefully that I didn't want to disturb you."

"Is something bothering you?"

"No. Just couldn't sleep, that's all." He brushed those errant strands of hair behind my ear. "Go on—eat your breakfast. Don't worry about me."

He managed to smile, but I could tell something was eating at him. I ate a few bites of food as he sat on the bed next to me and watched.

"Mmm ... delicious. I could get used to this."

Raising an eyebrow, he asked, "Is that so?" He leaned in and kissed my cheek.

"Yes."

Sometimes—especially when he was being this gentle and sweet—it was really difficult to believe that he was this tough homicide detective working some of the roughest neighborhoods in New York City. God, I loved this man. After my experience with that cheating ex-husband of mine, I never thought that I would ever let my heart be open to love again.

Andre's three-bedroom apartment was not a typical bachelor's pad. It was clean and tidy and rather spacious for New York City. His place was tastefully decorated with modern furniture and plenty of artwork, and he had transformed one of the bedrooms into an office. It was, however, nothing as grand as his father's place on Long Island.

Something occurred to me as I thought back to Andre's parents' anniversary party and his demeanor around Monica, his father's wife. There seemed to have been some tension between them, and I wanted to know why. I put down my fork and placed the tray in the center of the bed. Although I had been starving earlier, my stomach felt full halfway through the meal. I turned toward Andre. "I know this is off-topic and may seem to be coming from out of the blue, but the day we were at your father's house, I noticed that tension between you and Monica. If you don't mind my asking, did something happen between you two?"

He studied me for a moment, frowning. "Do we really need to talk about Monica?"

"No, we don't *need* to talk about her, but the tension between you two was so thick I could've cut it with a knife. I was just wondering about the reason for it. But if you don't want to talk about it, I'll respect your wishes."

"Good, then we won't."

"Why?"

"Didn't you just say that you would respect my wishes if I didn't want to talk about it?"

"I lied. Is there something I should know about you two?" I regretted the words almost as soon as they left my mouth. *Nice move, idiot.*

He glared at me long and hard." I can't believe you asked that, Nicole." He got up from the bed to leave the room. I called after him as he walked out of the room, but he only said, "I have work to do. You can show yourself out."

My tear-filled eyes shifted to a picture on his dresser—a photograph of a woman. It was eerie because, from a distance, I thought she resembled me. But it couldn't be me because I had never given Andre a picture of me. I got up from the bed and moved closer for a better view. Although the photo wasn't clear, I could see a definite resemblance between the woman in the picture and me.

I slipped my arms through Andre's robe and carried the picture to him. "Who's this?"

"I told you to show yourself out."

"No."

"No?"

"Not until I get some answers ..."

"You're not getting any. Goodbye, Nicole."

"Why won't you tell me who she is?"

"Leave," he said as he brushed past me.

I rolled my eyes at him. "Forget you, Andre, I'm going to find out." I looked at the picture again. It was old and fuzzy. *He wouldn't leave a picture around of another woman knowing that I will see it.* I stared down at the picture longer. The woman was wearing a floral printed sleeveless dress. The dress appeared dated.

Wait a minute.

This has got to be his mother.

Ugh!

How stupid, Nikki.

CHAPTER 13

Two days passed without any contact from Andre. I attempted to reach out to him once more by phone but was unsuccessful. He didn't respond to any of my voicemail messages. I decided that I wasn't going to try to contact him again. He had made it clear that he didn't want to talk to me, and I wasn't going to waste my time. I wish that I had not been so quick to jump to conclusions over that photo.

I busied myself with work in order to keep my thoughts from Andre and the mysteries surrounding him. Since the newspaper had received financial backing from several investors, it meant more work had started to flow in. I had come to enjoy my job at *News Today*. I was happy the newspaper had received enough financial assistance to keep its doors open and, most of all, keep me employed.

As I cleared my desk of some research printouts I had used for an article I was writing, my mind wandered to those two girls who had been murdered at the Lincoln Houses. About a week ago—*which now seems like months*—Andre had mentioned that the police thought they might have a lead on the killer, but I couldn't get anyone at the precinct to talk to me about any of it. Everything was so hush-hush.

And when the knife used to stab the girls was found by a homeless man last night, I couldn't understand the homeless man's involvement. A beat cop named Whitaker explained that the police had been called because a man waving a knife was threatening to cut some teenagers who had been taunting him as he tried to sleep on a bench outside one of the apartment buildings. When the police tried to confiscate the knife, the man had initially resisted giving it to them, muttering something about the knife belonging to him because he found it when it dropped from "the man's bag" when "the man" ran down the stairway of a building where he had been resting while trying to escape the scorching heat. He had pointed in the direction of the building where the latest murder victim, Andrea Brown, was discovered on the rooftop. Whitaker had questioned the man further and surmised that it could possibly have happened on the day of the murder. The police brought the man to the precinct for further questioning but released him because there had been no solid evidence to justify holding him. Off the record, Whitaker had revealed to me that the police lab was working on finding a DNA match with the murder victims using traces of blood found on the handle of the knife. They were also looking in the Combined DNA Index System (CODIS) for a possible DNA match with the killer.

I was startled out of my thoughts by the loud sound of my cell phone ringtone. I must have forgotten to put it on vibrate as I normally do when I'm at work. I found it odd that my mother's cell phone number was showing in the display. She almost never used her cell phone, and she rarely called me on mine.

"Hello, Mom."

"Nikki?" Her voice sounded shaky.

"Yes, Mom, what is it? Is everything okay?" I felt a knot growing in my stomach.

"It's your father, honey ..." She started crying and babbling words that I couldn't make out.

"Mom, calm down. Take a deep breath and tell me what's going on."

"Darling, he's gone!" she cried out.

"What do you mean, he's gone? Gone where?" Tears welled in my eyes. I knew what she meant, but I didn't want to accept it.

143

"Your father had a massive heart attack, darling. The ambulance came, but they weren't able to save him."

"No! That can't be! Mom, Dad was a healthy man! For God's sake, he's a cardiologist!"

Several coworkers had started to gather, staring at me. I didn't care because my world as I knew it had just changed in that instant. All I could think of was that I'd never see my dad alive again. I'd never be able to tell him how much I love him. I'd never hear him call me "my little darling" again or see his smile. This wasn't fair. Why him? *Why God? Why did you take my dad away from me?*

Janice rushed from her cubicle and gestured to our coworkers to disperse. She walked over to me and wrapped her arms around me tightly while I sat at my desk and cried uncontrollably. She took the phone from my hand and spoke into the receiver softly for a few moments before she ended the call.

I fell into Janice's opened arms and sobbed. *What I'm I going to do? Why did you have to leave me, Daddy?*

CHAPTER 14

The day of my father's funeral in Charlotte, it poured down rain. My mother used to say that when it rained on a wedding day, it meant that the couple would be blessed. Never heard what it meant for a funeral.

Dad was well-known in the community, so the church was filled with people there to pay their respects. Beautiful flower arrangements bloomed around his casket as well as in other areas of the church. It all felt surreal as I sat in the front row next to Mom and my aunts and uncle. Mom and I held hands, trying to comfort one another as the pastor spoke. She seemed to have more strength than I ever imagined she would at a time like this. My heart was broken for her—and for me. I couldn't stop thinking that this was all only a dream I'd wake up from. I had initially planned to go up to the podium to say a few words, just as the others had done who had spoken so eloquently about him, but I couldn't gather the strength to do so. My heart was too heavy, and tears filled my eyes, so I rested my head on my mother's shoulder while I held her hand and listened to others talk about my father.

My thoughts drifted to fun memories of my dad and me spending time together when I was a little girl. One of my fondest memories was the day he taught me how to ride a bicycle. He wanted to hold on to the bicycle as I pedaled, but I refused to let him. I wanted to show him that I knew how to do it on my own. After falling from my bicycle a gazillion times, he was so proud of me when I finally got the hang of it and rode my bike without any help. We celebrated by going out for ice cream ...

"Rocky Road, Nikki?"

"Mama only lets me have vanilla."

"Ah, I think today you deserve some Rocky Road for all your bumps and bruises."

"What if I want mint chocolate chip?"

That was my daddy's favorite.

"Nikki, baby, you can have whatever you like ..."

Whatever I like.

I want my daddy back.

******

We were exiting the church when I heard a familiar voice call my name. I couldn't believe it. That two-timing, cheating bastard had the audacity

146

to show up at my father's funeral. I continued to walk with my mom out of the church, not acknowledging him until my mom, southern belle that she is, nudged me. She gave me an all-too-familiar look which told me to use good manners. Had she forgotten what this son of a bitch had done? Had she forgotten that I had walked in on him having sex with my best friend—in *my* fucking bed? I refrained from saying what I would really have liked to have said to Michael and instead, nodded my head demurely.

"Hello, Nikki. How have you been? I'm so sorry about your dad."

I narrowed my eyes at him then turned to my mother, smiled at her sweetly. "Excuse us, please."

Before she could respond, two older women I wasn't familiar with walked over to greet her. Each of them gave her a kiss on the cheek and a hug as she watched me move down the church steps with Michael. The rain had stopped, but dark clouds still hovered above. Quite a few people had gathered outside the church. I offered a soft smile to a few and nodded as we passed by. There seemed to be some puzzled looks from some of the people who knew of our divorce.

Once we were several feet from the others near the parking lot, I stopped and glared at him. "What the *hell* do you think you're doing, Michael? You have no right to be here!"

He raised both his hands. "Nikki, look. I was very close to your father when we were married. He was like a father to me. I'm here because I wanted to pay my respects."

"That still gives you *no* right to be here. The service is over now. *Leave*." I looked around. "At least your whore had the good sense not to show up."

"Nikki, I want to apologize to you for—"

"Seriously?" I interrupted. "Just leave, Michael. I've heard your excuses before. I'm in no mood to revisit them. This isn't the time or the place. Besides, we're not married anymore. And thank God for that. Whatever you have to say has no effect on me. Don't try to soothe your guilty conscience by apologizing to me, especially now."

I attempted to walk away, but Michael grabbed my arm. "Nikki please, just hear me out," he pleaded.

I yanked my arm from his grip. "No. I don't listen to lies."

Michael reached for my hand. "Please, Nikki, I—"

"Is there a problem here?"

I whirled around and saw Andre, who towered over Michael by a few inches. I had almost forgotten how gorgeous a man he was. Our eyes locked and for a brief moment, everyone and everything around me disappeared. He spoke again, bringing me out of my catatonic state.

"Nicole? Are you all right?" he asked, his eyes soft.

"Andre, how did you—"

"This doesn't concern you, man," Michael interrupted.

Andre stepped close to Michael. "It does because Nicole concerns me."

Michael looked up briefly. "Nikki and I were having a conversation that does *not*—"

"I didn't see a conversation," Andre interrupted. "I saw an attempted assault. Put your hands on Nicole again and you won't be able to use your hands for a year."

"Who is this guy?" Michael asked me.

"My ..." I looked into Andre's eyes. "My boyfriend."

Andre nodded.

"Whatever, man." Michael backed away, stumbled into the front bumper of a Buick, and vanished into the parking lot.

I looked at the sidewalk. "You just ... showed up here."

"When I couldn't reach you, I contacted the

paper, and they told me what happened. Are you sure you're okay? Who was that guy harassing you?"

"My job wouldn't normally give out information like that. How did you find out? And how did you know exactly where to find me?" I tried to dig deeper.

"Remember, I'm a detective—I know how to find things out." He smiled slyly. "Again, who was that asshole?"

"That asshole, as you aptly put it, is my ex-husband, Michael."

He took my hand in his. "Baby, I'm so very sorry for all that's happened. I tried to call you as soon as I heard about your father, but you didn't pick up. I can't blame you for not wanting to talk to me after the way I treated you."

"But Andre, I called you several times," I said. "I *did* want to speak to you."

"I'm, um, sorry about that," Andre said. "You see, I ..." His eyes drifted away from my face.

My mother appeared and looped her arm into mine. "Darling, who is this handsome gentleman?" *My mom—a charmer even at a time like this.*

"Mom, this is Andre."

"Andre," she said slowly as if attempting to recall the name.

I had never really talked to her much about him

for obvious reasons. "*Detective* Andre, Mom," I reminded her.

"Ahh, so this is the New York detective you've told me about," she said, looking him over.

I'm sure it made him uncomfortable, but his expression gave nothing away.

"Well, it's so nice to meet you ... Detective." She extended her hand to him and offered her cheek.

"Likewise," he responded as he bent to kiss her.

A smile touched my lips as Andre and Mom both seemed to be enjoying each other's company. Mom was grilling him about his family and background and work, but he didn't seem to mind at all. She was quite impressed to learn that his father was a self-made real estate tycoon. She was even more impressed that Andre had jetted here to be with me today. Once in a while during their conversation, she would glance at me with an approving smile.

Andre had only taken a few hours off and needed to get back to New York. I walked with him to a limousine that had been parked at the curb, waiting for him. He closed the distance between us and clasped his arms around my waist. He gazed at me intensely, lowered his mouth to my lips, and brushed his lips lightly across mine. I parted my mouth, and he slid his tongue in, deepening the kiss. After, he raised my chin with his hand and said softly, "I missed you, baby. I don't ever want to lose you."

He kissed my forehead and entered the car. He waved and blew a kiss as the limo drove off.

******

The days following my dad's burial were spent helping my mom get organized in what would become her new life without him. There were times at night when I could hear her sobbing softly as I passed her bedroom door. I wanted to go in and wrap my arms around her and comfort her, but I didn't want to intrude on those private moments when she needed to soothe herself. My heart ached for her. Although she tried to convince me she would be fine, I contemplated returning to Charlotte to be near her. But who was I kidding? I would have been miserable moving back after having assimilated into the culture of a city like New York. I thought maybe I could convince her to move to New York, but I knew that wouldn't work, either, because she would be just as miserable living in New York as I would be living in North Carolina.

And I wouldn't have Andre or an exciting job tracking down a murderer ...

CHAPTER 15

I awakened feeling excited because Andre would be flying in from New York today. I had barely slept last night—all I could think about was how much I missed him and how good it felt when we were together.

On the other hand, I felt guilty about having to leave my mom while she was still going through a rough time dealing with the loss of my dad. My boss had allowed me only a short amount of time off since the paper had been super busy, and the front page needed my stories on the unresolved murder cases to continue boosting sales. I invited Mom to come back with me to New York for a couple of months, but she refused. She tried hard to assure me that she was fine. Although she promised that she would call me if she needed me for anything, I intended to call her as much as possible to make sure she was okay.

Since the day of my dad's funeral where I had introduced Mom to Andre, I got the feeling that the wheels in her head had been spinning. Her focus seemed to have shifted from nagging me into coming back home to nagging me into becoming a wife and mother. She had already warned me that I needed to get back to New York and "get things moving with that handsome young man"— her way of telling me to get the marriage talk started. She had admitted to being fond of Andre, and I smiled when I thought back to her saying that he didn't look like a typical police detective. When I asked her what she meant by that, she said she couldn't explain. She expressed to me how charming she thought he was and surprisingly did not bring up the fact that his father was a wealthy man. I believe that Andre had won her over just by being the awesome man that he is. I wonder how Dad would have perceived him. I thought he would have liked him very much.

I lingered in bed a few minutes more and listened to the sounds of birds chirping outside the window, which has become a rare experience for me now that I'm living in New York. I used to enjoy waking up in the morning to the chirping sounds when I lived here. My old bedroom looked much the same as it did when I left home to marry Michael, except for a few pieces of updated furniture and a remodeling of the adjacent bathroom. After graduating from Duke University, my intention was to move out of my parents' home and into an apartment, but my parents thought it would be a good idea to live at home for a while rather than rushing into finding a place of my own.

I had met Michael while attending Duke. He was a sophomore, and I was a freshman. Although he graduated a year before me, he stayed to attend Duke's law school. Our relationship blossomed over a period of time, and by the time he had graduated with his law degree, we were engaged to be married. It all seemed like such a lifetime ago.

I got out of bed, stretched, and yawned. I missed waking up to Freddie sleeping at the foot of my bed. Joann was taking care of him while I was away. I was sorry that neither of them was able to attend my father's funeral, but I understood their circumstances. They both felt horrible about it, but I would have been too busy to spend any real time with them anyway.

I showered and put on my running gear and stopped by the kitchen to grab a banana before I headed out the door for a long run. Mom was up already and in the kitchen. The delicious smell of an apple pie baking filled the air. She tried to convince me to stay and have a *decent* breakfast, but I refused. I had this great need to get out and get some fresh air.

I took in the familiar scenery of the brightly lit sky, greenery, cardinals, bluebirds, and a few woodpeckers as I jogged the pathways leading to a wooden boardwalk over a creek. I stopped for a moment to absorb all of the beauty I had taken for granted while growing up here. Although I'd seen it many times before, I felt like I was truly seeing it all for the first time.

While jogging back to the house, I remembered that Andre had mentioned he wanted to take Mom and me out to dinner so that we could all spend a little time together before he and I flew to New York. We were going back in his father's private jet, which was a good thing since it would mean that we wouldn't have to rush through dinner. Andre wasn't familiar with the restaurants in Charlotte, so he had left it up to me to make the reservations. Mom and I both loved the food at Blue Restaurant, a lovely Mediterranean restaurant. I was sure Andre would love it, too.

******

Mom and I gathered together some of Dad's clothing for charity as we waited on Andre's arrival. I had offered to pick him up from the airport, but he said that he would have a limousine waiting to drive him here. He insisted that I use the time to spend with my mother since we would be leaving after dinner. The task of going through Dad's things had to be difficult for Mom. I was glad I was there to help her sort through his things rather than her having to do it alone.

"Mom, are you sure you're up to doing this right now?" I asked, covering one of her hands with mine.

"Yes, darling, I'm fine," she replied. "Are you okay with it, sweetie?" She searched my face.

"I am. It just saddens me that I will never see Daddy wear these clothes again." My eyes filled with tears.

She leaned in and kissed my forehead. "I know, darling. Me, too. Hey, are you excited to see that tall, handsome man of yours?" She smiled, swiftly changing the subject.

"Oh yes," I said as I wiped a tear away. "So tell me, Mom, what do you think of him? Honestly?"

She looked up at me from where she knelt, taping one of the boxes we had just filled with clothing. "So far, he seems like a great guy. When you first mentioned you were dating a police detective, I had my doubts. But he doesn't seem at all like those hot shot detectives I've seen on TV."

"Mom, you can't compare a real person with actors on the television shows you watch." I shook my head and giggled.

"Darling, I believe that there is some truth in

those character types. Well, anyway, he seems like a sweet, good-natured man and a true gentleman. I can tell by the way he looks at you that he loves you." She had a dreamy look in her eyes. I guessed she was thinking about her early days with Dad.

"Really? I mean, it shows that much?"

"Yes, honey, and it shows equally on you."

She got up and walked over to the closet to close the double doors. She then took a seat on the cushioned bench at the foot of her bed and patted the other side, gesturing for me to sit next to her. She took one of my hands and placed it between both of hers. "Sweetheart, if you love this man like I sense that you do, you've got to stop holding back and give him a chance."

"What makes you think I'm not giving him a chance? I've already told him I love him, Mom." I'd really had no intention of getting this deep in conversation with Mom about my relationship with Andre. What had come over me?

"That may be so, honey. I'm not disputing whether or not you've said those words to one another, but I do know the hurt you suffered from, with all that mess that went on with Michael. Just because you say the words doesn't necessarily mean that your heart has healed. Your heart may still be wounded, but you've got to let go of that hurt completely so that you can move on. This fellow, Detective Andre, really loves you, honey."

I bit my lip, pondering what she had just said. *Am I really holding back? If Mom had noticed it, had Andre also sensed it? I really do love him. I guess it's true that I've never forgiven Michael for his indiscretions. How in the world do you forgive a person you hate?*

"Honey, I've heard you use the word hate on many occasions in regards to Michael. I know it's hard to forgive someone who's hurt you in that way—especially the betrayal of someone you loved and trusted." She lifted my chin with her hand, and my eyes filled with tears again as I remembered the hurt of my past. "I'm not saying that by forgiving him you have to communicate with him or erase what he did to you. What I'm trying to say is that the forgiveness is for *you*, darling, not for him. It helps you to move on with your life and put the past behind you." She gently wiped a tear away from my eye.

I would never have thought that opening up to Mom would help me find insight into my unresolved feelings about my past relationship as well as help me understand why I haven't been able to move forward in my current relationship.

The loud sound of the doorbell startled the both of us. "That must be your young man. Honey, you go and freshen up your face while I get the door." She walked out of the bedroom.

I went into the bathroom and patted my eyes with tissues and freshened up my makeup before I went downstairs to greet Andre. I hoped he wouldn't notice the puffiness under my eyes.

I heard the comforting sounds of Mom and Andre engaging in congenial conversation as I descended the staircase to the main level of my parents beautiful French-style home. When I entered the living room, Andre stood and gazed lovingly at me, touching my soul and sending a renewed feeling of warmth all through my body. Since my talk with Mom, it was as though I was seeing him with a brand new heart. I felt my love for him deepen. I smiled brightly as he quickly moved toward me and encircled his arms around me, kissing me passionately.

"I missed you, babe," he whispered in my ear.

I had almost forgotten that my mom was present, but she didn't seem to mind our display of affection. My face flushed with embarrassment as I glanced over at her. She beamed with joy.

Andre caught on to my embarrassment. "Excuse me, Mrs. Watkins, but I've missed your beautiful daughter immensely and was overcome with happiness."

My mother smiled and stood. "Well, are we all ready to go? I'm going to get my purse."

The restaurant was already filled with other patrons when we arrived. Since I had called ahead for reservations, we didn't have to wait to be seated. I watched Andre scan the menu with a puzzled look.

"What's wrong?" I asked.

"Oh, nothing," he responded, grinning.

"You look confused."

"I'm trying to figure out what I should order. Any suggestions?"

I moved closer to him and explained some of the foods on the menu he was unfamiliar with. I ordered my favorite dish, *kushari*, an Egyptian dish of rice, chick peas, macaroni, and lentils topped with a tomato sauce. Mom ordered lamb with fresh salad. Andre decided to try the *kushari*, too.

"So, Andre, do you like children?" Mom asked.

"Yes, I love children. I hope to be a father someday." He smiled.

"How many children would you like?"

Andre sipped from his glass of water. "I'm not sure."

"I had Nicole when I was only twenty-two. Nicole's not getting any younger..." She glanced at me.

"Mom." I interrupted.

"Tell me, Andre, do you see yourself being a detective all your life?"

"It suits me for now."

When dinner was over, we were chauffeured back to the house to drop Mom off and pick up my luggage. It was difficult for me to leave Mom.

"Mom, are you sure you're going to be okay?"

"As much as I enjoyed you being here with me baby, I know that you have your life to get back to. I'm going to be fine." Her eyes filled with tears.

I grabbed her and hugged her tight. "If you need me you call me. You hear?" I pulled back to see her face. A tear rolled down my cheek.

She nodded. "I will."

I wiped away her tears with my thumb. "I promise I'll keep in touch with you often."

Andre tried to convince her to come to New York for a short visit soon since she wasn't interested in moving there. She promised she would think about it. We hugged and kissed her goodbye then headed to the limo to be driven to the airport.

"I like your mother very much," Andre said.

"She certainly likes you." *Is now the time to ask him about the picture of his mother on his dresser? He seems so happy.*

"Sorry she interrogated you so much."

"It's okay," Andre said. "My mother used to do

the same thing. Where are you going? Who are you going to be with? When will you be back? I think I learned my questioning techniques from her. And you"—he kissed my nose—learned to be so inquisitive because of your mother."

CHAPTER 16

When I entered the jet, I was absolutely amazed at the luxurious interior. I don't know what I expected since I'd never been inside a jet before. Although it was a small one, the inside seemed quite large. It was furnished with six plush tan leather seats which reclined into beds. A colorful geometric print fabric adorned the throw pillows on each of the chairs. The floor was carpeted in a thick cream-colored Berber. There were two flat-screen television monitors secured to a ledge that ran along either side of the interior and tabletops that slid out from the walls on either side that could be used for dining. Andre escorted me to one of the seats and sat in another facing me.

"Wow, this is beautiful!" I ran my hands across the soft, tan leather of the chair.

"It's okay, I guess." He shrugged. "Would you like something to drink?"

"No, thank you."

The pilot instructed us to buckle up and prepare for takeoff. Upon takeoff, I was initially a bit nauseated by the smell of jet fuel, and I also had to become accustomed to the sound of the engine.

I caught Andre's eye when I turned toward him after admiring the view outside the window. His stare was intense. "Everything okay?" I asked.

"I'm fine," he answered. "I was just thinking about how much I love you—and how much I miss you when we're not together."

I ignored my inner self, which silently screamed for me to repeat those words back to him. Instead, I swallowed hard.

"Nicole, I want to explain to you why I got upset that day in my apartment when you questioned me about Monica."

"Andre, I was wrong for asking you. I apologize."

He looked at me with gentle eyes. "No, baby, there's no need for you to apologize. I should have told you about what happened between Monica and me."

"Something ... happened?" I asked in a small voice.

"Are you kidding me? She's my father's wife, Nicole. What kind of person do you think that I am?" He frowned.

"You just said that something happened between the two of you," I retorted.

He ran his hand through that beautiful mass of thick hair, staring at me with frustration. "Okay, I admit that was a poor choice of words. Something did happen, but it was a long time ago, and I wasn't a voluntary participant."

"What do you mean by that? And how long ago was it?" I shifted in my seat.

"I'm going to get to all of that if you'll just listen without interrupting, please."

His cell phone rang. *Damn it! Of all the times for his freaking phone to ring!*

"Hold on a minute—I have to get this. It's someone from work."

My lips pressed into a thin, hard line while I waited for his phone call to end.

He pressed a button on his phone to answer. "Detective Moore."

Judging from his expression, it seemed the news was neither good nor bad.

"When did he come in? Is he sure? Why didn't Kowalski and Harris ask him that when he *first* came in? We've lost a few days, man. Okay, okay, keep me informed. I'm headed back to New York as we speak. Yes, absolutely. Grill him, all right? Bye." He tapped a button to end the call, and a frown spread across his face as he looked over at me.

"Good news, I hope?" I raised my eyebrows.

"Yes and no, but it might be too soon to discuss it with you," he teased.

"What happened?"

"This is off the record for now. Understand?"

"Andre, you should know by now that I won't report anything I'm not given permission to report. I thought I'd already made that clear."

"Remember that homeless man I told you about? The one brought in for questioning some time ago?"

"The one who found the murder weapon?" I asked.

"Yes. Well, he decided on his own to go back to the police precinct to see if he could get *his* knife back."

"What?" I asked, giggling. "Didn't he realize that once the police took it, it became evidence in a murder case?"

"I know, but get this. He thought if he gave a description of the murderer, the police would give him the knife back."

"Are you telling me he saw what the killer looked like and never told the police when he was taken in before? Could he be lying about seeing the killer in order to get the knife back?"

"Well, from what I understand, when he was brought in the first time, the detectives on duty didn't do a thorough job of questioning him. No one asked him for a detailed description. He gave some basics—approximate height, weight, body type. He also described what the person was wearing. But he never gave a description of facial features or any other details. I'm willing to bet that he either skated around the issue or wasn't asked about any distinguishing features."

"I can't believe a police department would be that inefficient."

"Not a police department, Kowalski and Harris. They're old-timers waiting on their pensions. Anyway, it seems the homeless man is at the precinct right now giving a detailed description of the man he saw running from the scene the day of the murder. There's a forensic sketch artist interviewing him as we speak. I'm hoping that once the picture is released to the public, it will lead to an arrest."

"Of course, you know I'd like an exclusive," I said with a coy smile.

"That all depends on how nice you are to me, Ms. Watkins." He winked and gave me his signature smile.

I deliberately cleared my throat, "Now can we get back to the matter at hand? You and Monica?"

I smiled sweetly to ease the transition back to our earlier topic.

"Oh right, I almost forgot about that," he said solemnly. "Where was I?"

"How long ago did this happen?" I was eager to get on with it.

He stared into space for a moment, seemingly trying to recall a memory. "I think it was about seven or eight years ago. My father was away on a business trip. At that time, I was still living at the house but was in the process of finding an apartment of my own. I thought I was too old to be staying in my father's house, and I felt awkward living in the house with him and his new wife—he and Monica had married three years earlier. The other issue was that it was a long commute into Manhattan every day." He sighed. "I've always had a feeling that Monica had a little crush on me."

Andre searched my face, trying to read my expression, but I gave nothing away. He continued.

"That's one of the reasons I've always made sure to keep my distance from her. Anyway, I came in late one night. It was my day off, and I'd had a few drinks with some of the guys. Monica was still up when I came into the house. She made some small talk with me, said she was feeling restless and thought that she'd make herself a drink. She asked me to have one with her. Against my better judgment—my judgment was off anyway due to having drinks earlier—I agreed. I made the mistake of letting her fix my drink. We finished our drinks while chatting a little. I'd started feeling really exhausted, so I left her in the living room and went upstairs to bed. When I woke the next morning, I discovered her next to me in my bed."

"Hmm, let me see ... and you *don't* know how she got there, right?" I asked. "You expect me to believe that?"

"Listen, Nicole, you wanted to know what happened, so I'm telling you. Do you or don't you want to know more?" he asked, his face tight with tension.

"Yes," I said. "Please tell me how your stepmother ended up in bed with you without your knowledge."

"Trust me, I'm not proud of what happened, nor am I comfortable telling you about it, but you deserve to know." He shifted his eyes from me to the intertwining fingers of his hands. "I didn't *know* how she got there. I was knocked out by the time my head hit the pillow. I don't remember a thing after that. I asked her what she was doing in my bed. At first, she made up a lie—and I could tell she was lying. I threatened her into telling me the truth. She finally admitted she had drugged my drink so I wouldn't remember the act."

"What act?" I asked, already knowing the answer.

"You know, having sex with her." He grimaced.

"You had ... sex with your stepmother? Oh my God, Andre!"

"Baby, *she* had sex with *me*," Andre said. "While I was drugged."

"But how could ... how could you perform if you were drugged?"

"I don't know, okay?"

"I can't believe this," I said. "This ... this kind of thing ..." I couldn't stop shaking my head. "I am so ... confused."

"Baby, I was furious and confused. I would have arrested her on the spot for rape if not for my father."

"Is that all?"

"What do you mean?"

"Big, burly, strong cop raped by his stepmother," I said. "Your career would have ended immediately."

"Yeah." He looked away. "It probably would have."

"Did you tell him? Does he know what happened?"

He hung his head. "No, he doesn't know anything."

"He has to have noticed the tension between you two. I noticed it from the start." I stared at him dubiously, finding it all so hard to believe. "Why haven't you told him?"

"Because it would have destroyed him, and I couldn't hurt him that way. It took him a long while to get over the murder of my mother, and unfortunately, he truly loves that slut. I don't want to be the one to break his heart again." He clenched his teeth. "Of course he notices the tension between Monica and me. He's asked me on several occasions about it. He thinks it's because I think she's a gold digger and I disapprove of the huge age difference between them. He also thinks that since I've put my mother on such a pedestal, no other woman in his life will ever be good enough."

Silence pervaded the air. I reached out, grabbed his hand, and held it gently between mine. "Look at me. I don't blame you for what she did to you. It wasn't your fault, baby." *Did I just call him "baby"? I did, and my inner self is so pleased.* "She tricked you into having sex with her. I think your father deserves to know what type of person he's married to."

"Nicole, I was just as much to blame as she was. I should not have taken another drink after already having a few beforehand. Besides, this happened so long ago, and nothing like it has ever happened since. He and Monica seem to be doing fine—and he's happy. I don't want to destroy that. I also don't want Katie having to grow up without both parents as I did."

"I understand that, but ..." I took a deep breath. *Could it be?* "How long ago did this happen?"

"Seven, eight years ago," he said. "I'm trying to forget it ever happened, okay?"

Katie. Katie is seven. Could she be ... No. That's too horrible to imagine! And I'm sure Andre has already considered this possibility. Hasn't he?

He got up from his seat, knelt in front of me, and pressed a finger against my lips. "I don't want to talk about it anymore. It's a closed subject. Okay?"

I nodded, and he covered my lips with his mouth. Our tongues began to do their dance. He reached inside my blouse and cupped my breast with his hand, massaging it and twisting my nipple between his fingers. And then the pilot announced the seatbelt precautions.

"We'll continue this later," he said in a husky voice. He returned to his seat and buckled his belt.

"Andre, there's something else I've been meaning to ask you." I hoped my uneasiness didn't show.

"What's the question?" His eyebrows raised, curiosity in his eyes.

"There is a picture of a woman on the dresser in your bedroom." I described it. "Who is she?"

"That's my mother."

I caught my breath. "Your mother?"

"Yes."

"Oh. She's, um, she's beautiful." I smiled. "I thought she might have been your mother."

"Then why ask about it?"

I wished I had never asked! "Well, at the time, there was, um, there is a striking resemblance between her and me."

"Okay. And?"

I closed my eyes. "Did you ... did you get involved with me because I remind you of your mother?"

"Nicole, that's ridiculous!" he sputtered. "Why would you think something like that?"

"Your father stared at me like he had seen a ghost when I first met him. Now that I think of it, I saw the two of you whispering. Is that what you were whispering about? How much I look like your mother?"

We were interrupted by the pilot's announcement about the landing. Andre's eyes flashed and he frowned. "What are you talking about? You're not making any sense," he growled.

Before I could respond, the door to the jet flew open. Two airport security men entered along with a chubby man with a cocky facial expression dressed in a rumpled black suit and holding a badge in his hand. He shoved the badge into Andre's face. "Are you Detective Andre Moore?"

Andre seemed just as confused as I was. "Yes, I'm Detective Moore. How can I help you?"

"You need to come with us," he commanded.

"Who are you and why do you want me to come with you?" Andre demanded.

I started to feel scared. I had a really bad feeling about this.

"Detective, I'm warning you. Don't make this any harder than it has to be. Now come along with us."

"I'm not going anywhere until you tell me what the hell is going on. I'm a New York City homicide detective, and the least you can do is extend courtesy to a fellow police officer."

The chubby detective turned to the two airport security men who were standing close behind him then returned his attention to Andre, a smug look on his face.

"As you wish," he said sarcastically. "I'm homicide detective Tom Collins of the Special Victims Squad here in Queens. You're under arrest for the rape and murder of Andrea Brown." Then he read Andre his Miranda rights while one of the two security men put handcuffs on him.

"Get your hands off me!" Andre shouted as he struggled to break loose from the man's hold.

I sprang from my seat. "Why are you doing this to him? He's done nothing!"

"Lady, calm down," Collins said. "This is police business."

The other security man moved quickly to help his partner hold Andre until the cuffs were on him.

"I didn't murder anybody!" Andre shouted.

CHAPTER 17

All hell broke loose after Andre's arrest.

Someone had tipped off CNN, and the blinding glare of cameras greeted Andre as the detective led Andre through the terminal. A swarm of police and the crush of reporters kept me far from him.

I found a place to sit in a waiting area to catch my breath.

And try to find my sanity.

I felt helpless, but most of all, I was devastated. I didn't know what to do or what to think. Could my beloved Andre have been the rapist and murderer of Andrea Brown? Could he have also raped and murdered Vanessa Rojas? It just didn't make sense to me. I felt nauseous and dizzy. The motion of the crowds of people and the noise didn't help.

I dove into my memory banks, trying to remember—the times we had discussed the cases, the murder scenes, the expressions on Andre's face as he briefed me on the details of each case. I couldn't find any clue pointing to him. Was it because he was so efficient at committing the crimes and eliminating evidence? My heart told me that he could not have committed such heinous crimes, but my brain told me to remember that things were not always as they seemed. *Anyone* was capable of committing murder.

I reached into my purse for my cell phone. I needed to contact Blackman. I should be the one assigned to this story so I could stay close to Andre. I pushed the button to speed dial his office.

"Blackman," his voice boomed. I was taken aback when he answered instead of his secretary, Pam. Thank God I didn't have to waste time going through her.

"Mr. Blackman, I'm glad I was able to reach you. This is Nicole, I—"

"Ms. Watkins. I've been trying to reach you. I left you several messages to contact me. The police department put out a sketch of the man who murdered those two girls. My sources tell me the sketch is a picture of your detective friend, Andre Moore. Hold on!"

I heard a collision of voices growing louder.

"Holy shit!" Blackman shouted. "There he is on TV. Can you believe that son of a bitch was the rapist and murderer all along? And CNN has the scoop. Shit!"

"I know about the sketch, Mr. Blackman," I said, "because I was with him when he got arrested."

"What do you mean you were with him? Don't tell me you knew about this and kept it a secret."

I got up off the chair and moved to a more secluded area of the terminal near a service exit. "I had no idea, Mr. Blackman. In fact, Andre seemed as shocked as I was when they arrested him on the plane."

"You were on his daddy's private jet?"

"Yes. We were on our way back from North Carolina when he got the call about the sketch. Andre had *no* idea he was the person being sketched." *At this moment, my instincts are telling me there is much more to this.*

"Maybe he just pretended to be shocked," Blackman said.

"No, he was genuinely shocked, Mr. Blackman. I know him. I don't think he did this."

"They wouldn't have arrested him if they didn't have evidence."

True. "I think he's being framed, Mr. Blackman."

"I heard from a trusted source that his DNA is on the knife."

181

I swallowed hard. "That ... that can't be. How trusted is this source?"

"He's head of forensics," Blackman said. "He's unimpeachable."

Oh no! "Mr. Blackman, I would like to be assigned to—"

"Absolutely not! You're too involved with the suspect. I need someone who won't be biased."

"Please, Mr. Blackman," I pleaded. "I promise you won't be disappointed. Have I ever let you down? I'm *perfect* for this story because I have personal knowledge that no other reporter will be privy to."

"Watkins, you're killing me. No pun intended." He sighed. "The *first* sign I see of you screwing up, I'm pulling you from the story. Do you understand me?"

"Yes, sir. I won't let you down, but how will I get to Andre?"

"I'll have to cash in a few favors to get you some face time with Andre, but you'll get your interview."

"Do you know where they're taking him?"

"His own precinct," Blackman said. "Ironic, isn't it? You're on the clock as of now. Get going."

Click.

I looked at my phone and noticed several missed calls, including calls from Janice and Joann. I presumed that somehow they had also heard the news. I quickly sent them texts to let them know I was fine and would talk with them later.

Two hours later, I entered Andre's precinct. Several of the officers greeted me as I entered, remembering me from my personal or professional visits with Andre. I was escorted to Andre's cell. He sat motionless on a thin mattress, his elbows propped on his knees and holding his head, which was pointed toward the floor. I had never seen him look so lost or so sad. His beautiful hair was disheveled, and his eyes were bloodshot. He looked up as I approached his cell. He looked weary, his face showing signs of frustration, exhaustion, and fear.

"What are you doing here? You're the last person I expected."

"I convinced Blackman to assign me to the story," I responded.

He stood and moved to the bars of the cell. He reached out to touch me, but the officer on duty warned him that we couldn't have physical contact.

"Nicole, I *swear* I didn't do this," he said in anguish. "I don't know why that homeless man said he saw me."

I wasn't sure what to feel as I watched him go through this torment, but I knew I couldn't fall apart. I had to keep it together. And I had to remember that I was there to do a job, and I couldn't let my personal feelings get in the way. I was so conflicted—I didn't know whether I was facing my lover who I believed to be an innocent man or a complete stranger who was guilty as charged.

"The DNA found on the murder weapon matches your DNA."

"That's impossible!"

"The knife was the same murder weapon used to kill Vanessa Rojas, which means that your DNA was found on the weapon used to kill both girls." I glanced at the guard. "How do you explain that?" I whispered.

"What are you talking about? All of this is impossible!"

"Did you allow them to take a swab from you?"

"Yes, but only because I know that I didn't touch either of those girls, and I have nothing to hide."

"You're definitely going to need a good lawyer," I said. "Have you been in touch with your father yet?"

"Yes, he's sending a lawyer, and he's coming here as soon as he can. Dad was away on a business trip in Chicago when I called him."

"I'd like to interview the homeless man the police spoke with. Do you know where I can find him?" I pulled out my notebook.

"Nicole, Andrea Brown was murdered on the

day of my father's anniversary party. I was with you. How could I possibly have raped and murdered her?"

I knew he was desperately trying to prove his innocence, but as a reporter, I had to deal with facts. "That's true, Andre. We were together later in the day. But if you remember, the coroner's report stated she was murdered much earlier in the day."

"Are you telling me you don't believe me?" he hissed. "How can you believe I'd do something so horrific?" His face seemed to crumble.

"Listen, I understand your frustration, but you know as well as I do that we have to deal with the facts. Do you have any idea how your DNA got on that knife?"

"I've told you already, I don't know. I wasn't even with the officers the day they got it from the homeless man."

"Well, I'm going to locate him to see if I can get more information. There has to be something he didn't share with the police. I might be able to get him to trust me enough to share it with me. Have they officially charged you yet?"

"I'm being arraigned tomorrow. I'm sure they'll make a circus of it." He hung his head and then looked back up with such sadness in his eyes. "I'll have either my father or my lawyer give you the details of the arraignment in case you want to be there."

"Of course I want to be there. Give me the information now so I can contact one of them if I find out anything that might be useful."

He gave me his father's phone number but couldn't remember the name of the attorney his father retained. He also gave me a detailed description of the homeless man and told me where he usually hung out.

"For what it's worth," I said, "I think you're being framed."

"Yeah. But my DNA on the knife keeps you from *knowing* I'm being framed."

"Did you at any time handle that knife while it was in evidence?"

He shook his head. "No. Never went near it."

I signed. "I'm sure there's a logical explanation." I approached the bars. "I know we're not allowed to touch but—"

He reached through the bars, pulled me to him, and kissed me roughly on the lips. "What are they going to do, arrest me for kissing?"

I left the police station determined to find answers—not only for the story but also for myself.

As I weaved through the crowds on my way toward the Lincoln Houses, my brain was a whirlwind as it replayed conversations with Andre about the murder cases and his personal life. I tried to piece together information that would make some sense out of his connection to these murders, but I kept coming up short. It just didn't make any sense. Why would he do to those girls what had been done to his own mother? Why would he want to replicate a gruesome crime that haunted him to this day?

A few blocks from the subway station, I rounded a corner and saw in the near distance a man who fit the description Andre gave me. The man wore a dirty, faded green jacket with a food-stained yellow-white T-shirt under it, his worn blue jeans stained with dirt sat on a bench outside one of the Lincoln House's buildings. I was initially afraid to approach him but quickly decided there was too much resting on this—especially if he had information that could help my story as well as help Andre — *if* Andre was telling the truth about not killing those two young girls.

I turned and walked back down the street to the bodega on the corner by the subway station. Maybe food would help get him to talk to me.

After getting the man a meal and some coffee, my heart began to pound a little harder—not because I was afraid of the man hurting me, but because I was afraid of what he might have seen. What if he didn't know any more than what he had already told the police, or worse, what if he told me something that incriminated Andre even further? Well, there was no turning back now.

"Hello." I waved my hand at him in an attempt to grab his attention, but he responded with a blank stare. "My name is Nicole. How are you?" I smiled and opened the brown paper bag in front of him. "I hope you like egg and bacon bagels and coffee." I held the bag and coffee in front of me.

The man grabbed the bag and peeked inside then looked at me and gave me a toothless grin. "Thank you," he said as he tore at the paper around the bagel. After taking a bite, he looked up at me. "What you say your name is?"

"Nicole. What's yours?" I tried to use some of my southern charm.

"They call me Charlie." He sipped some coffee.

"Well, it's very nice to meet you, Charlie. May I sit down?" Without waiting for his response, I sat on the bench, keeping some distance between us. I didn't want to invade his personal space, and I was trying my best to avoid the malodorous air emanating from him.

"Charlie, may I ask you a question?" I watched the last of the bagel disappear into his mouth.

"I don't know, that all depends." He grimaced.

"I'm not sure what you mean."

"I mean, no, you can't ask me a damn thing if you the cops," he said sharply.

"Well, that's good—because I'm not the cops."

"Then go 'head and ask me. I'll let you know if I want to answer your question." He grinned. "You one fine lady." He winked at me.

"Charlie, I would like to ask you a few questions about the person you saw running away from the murder scene the day you found the knife that the police took from you."

"Look, lady, I already done told the police what I saw. You sure you not no cop?"

"I promise you I'm not a cop. I'm a reporter with the newspaper, and I just want to verify the story the police are telling about what happened."

"Newspaper reporter? That mean my picture's gonna be in the paper?" He grinned.

"I'll have to check with my boss about that, but your story will definitely be in the paper." I smiled.

"I already done told the police that that cop was the one I saw." He squashed the empty paper bag and twisted it in his hands.

"Yes, I know that. But can you tell me a little bit more about that cop? Is there anything else you can remember about him? Did he have any scars?

Or anything on any part of his body that you could see?"

"The police done asked me that already, and I told them what I saw. Why you keep asking me the same old questions the cops done already asked me? I'm tired of repeating myself. There ain't nothing that stood out." He stood. "Thanks for the food."

I couldn't let him get away. "What was he wearing again?"

"Shorts and a hoodie."

"Did you see anything unusual about ..."

Charlie blinked at me. "About a man's legs? Hey, lady, I ain't into that, okay?"

"I meant, were they skinny legs, muscular legs, tan legs, brown legs, black legs ..."

"Hey, wait a damn minute ... hot damn!" He clapped his hands, "There *is* something I saw. He had a big ole tattoo on one of his legs." He touched one side of his own leg to demonstrate. "You see, it was hot that day, and when he ran down them stairs, I saw that big ass tattoo." He started laughing. "And whoever did it, did a lousy job. I couldn't tell what it was supposed to be. Almost like they spilled the ink on him."

Because it might not have been a tattoo at all. It could have been a huge scar or even a birthmark. "Charlie, are you *sure* you saw a tattoo on one of his legs?"

190

"I'm sure."

"Which leg?"

"I don't remember which leg it was. I don't know ... maybe his right leg." He stared off into space. "I don't remember, but I do know that he had a big ass tattoo on his leg, and it looked more like a big black bruise than a tattoo."

"Would you recognize it if you saw it again?"

"Hell yes. Ugly as that thing was, I'd recognize it in a second." He grinned. "Think if I told the cops about the tattoo they'd give me my knife back?"

I had to think fast. "Um, no, but they might arrest you."

"For what?"

"For ... for withholding evidence." *Could they do that?* "You don't want to be arrested, do you?"

"No." Charlie rose from the bench and left in a hurry, leaving his coffee behind.

My thoughts went back to the dozens of times I had seen Andre's naked body. He had no birthmark or tattoo or scar at all on *any* part of his body. Oh my God, if Charlie was telling the truth, it could mean Andre was not the killer.

So if Andre wasn't the killer, who is the person Charlie saw that looked just like him?

And where was this killer now?

CHAPTER 18

Although it felt good to be back at work, I hadn't been looking forward to the pileup on my desk. I scowled at the mountain of files on my desk, stacked there while I was away attending my father's funeral.

Because I couldn't seem to keep my mind on anything other than what was happening with Andre, I pushed that mountain of files off my desk.

Janice peered around my cubicle. "Hey, is everything okay?"

"Trying to make files disappear."

"Wouldn't it be glorious if your method really worked? Is there anything that I can help with?"

"Not unless you're a magician."

"Okay. You know I only ask once." Janice laughed.

I spent the rest of the morning reviewing and editing the article I wrote on my interview with Charlie and sent it to Blackman. I tried to reach Andre's father several times—unsuccessfully. I wanted to share what Charlie told me about a birthmark on the leg of the man he had seen that day, in hopes it would be useful in Andre's case. I needed to know when and where Andre was going to be arraigned. If Andre's father didn't call me back soon, I was going to have to call the courthouse, and sometimes calling that "labyrinth of the law" was a lost cause.

The phone on my desk rang loudly, startling me. "Nicole Watkins, how may I help you?"

Silence.

I knew the person was still there because I heard breathing.

"Hello, may I help you?" I asked, this time with less cheerfulness.

"I have some information." The voice was obviously that of a man trying to disguise his voice.

"What kind of information do you have, sir?" I said matter-of-factly. We were used to getting prank calls like this at the paper every so often.

"It's about that cop that got arrested."

My throat suddenly became dry, and I tried to swallow. This person knew Andre and I had some sort of connection. Otherwise, he wouldn't have called me directly.

"Are you still there?" the voice asked.

"Yes, I'm here. What can you tell me about the cop?" I pressed the phone tightly against my ear.

"The cop? Funny. You mean your boyfriend."

I wasn't going to admit anything. "Do you have *any* information that—"

"Slow your roll, home girl. I'm on your side. I saw your man's picture, but I've also seen someone else that looks *just* like him."

"Sir, I'm sure there are a quite a few people around the city who fit the description of that police officer." I tried to be patient, twisting the cord of the telephone around my fingers, but I was also excited. If Andre's lawyer could produce this look-a-like, a jury would be hard-pressed to find Andre guilty.

"You're not hearing me, yo. I said that I've seen someone that looks *just* like him. He could be his twin."

Yes! "To whom am I speaking?"

"You trippin'," he growled. "I ain't crazy."

"I could be tracing this call." I looked at the Caller-ID. "I have your number right here, and I can—"

"This phone gonna be in the trash after I make this call," he interrupted.

He was using a burner? Why?

"Um, where can I see Andre's twin?"

195

The man laughed. "Yeah, *now* he's Andre. I can tell you where to find his twin."

I wasn't sure if I should believe him or not, but I didn't want him to get frustrated and hang up on me without me getting the information he allegedly had. "Where can I find him?" I picked up my pen and pulled off a sticky note.

"Two-thirty East One Hundred and Fifth."

Click.

"Damn it!" I hung up the phone. *What the hell is at that address?* I Googled the address.

Park East High School.

Oh my God! Is that where both girls sometimes went to school? But who am I supposed to be looking for?

Janice peeked her head around my cubicle wall. "You're being especially loud today, but I don't blame you for the noise. If *my* boyfriend was arrested for murder—"

"He didn't do it," I interrupted. I told her about the birthmark Charlie saw.

"Maybe Charlie only saw a shadow or something reflecting onto his leg," Janice said. "Or some mud or something."

"Near the Lincoln Houses? Nothing green grows there."

"Oh yeah."

"And I just hung up with an anonymous caller

who claims he's seen someone who looks like Andre." I grabbed my purse off my desk.

"What? I don't understand."

"I don't have time to explain. If Blackman comes looking for me, let him know that I'm on my way to check out a tip from an anonymous caller." I walked away, leaving her standing in the pathway between her cubicle and mine.

"Wait!" She caught up to me. "Where are you going? Please tell me you're not meeting up with some stranger who called you on the telephone? Are you crazy?"

"I'm not going to meet the caller. He said I should go to Park East High School. That's where I'm headed." I walked briskly away.

I hailed a taxi to drive me to the school. I needed to get there in a hurry and didn't have time to figure out the subway route. I pulled my cell phone from my purse to see if Andre's father had called. Nothing. It was just as well because I was not at all sure I would make it to the arraignment anyway.

As the taxi driver weaved in and out of traffic, I tried to come up with a valid reason for my visit to Park East. Many of the city high schools were now guarded to prevent violent incidents from occurring, and security was tight. As I was thinking up a plan, I remembered the day when Andre told me that both girls attended the same high school, but I couldn't seem to remember him telling me the name of the high school they attended.

I called Janice.

"Janice Kent speaking. How may I help you?"

"Janice, it's me. Can you do me a favor?"

"Of course! Name it."

"Can you do a little research and find out what high school Vanessa Rojas and Andrea Brown attended?"

"You think they attended Park East?" she asked.

"I'm not sure. Janice, please. I need this information as soon as possible."

"Okay, I'll get on it right now."

"Janice?"

"Yes?"

"Don't let anyone else know what you're doing."

"I won't."

"Thanks." I pushed the END button.

I began to feel a little adrenaline building. What if those girls did attend Park East High School? I was still not quite sure what I was supposed to find there, but somehow I knew it would be the piece I needed to solve this puzzle.

The taxi driver pulled up to the curb in front of the school. I paid him and got out. I stood there for a few moments, staring at the industrial brick building as a few kids milled about. The summer session was in, so they were most likely taking a break between classes. I walked past them and entered the lobby. A man in a security uniform sitting at a desk immediately asked if he could help me. I was a little nervous because I knew I was entering under false pretenses, and I wasn't sure if he would be able to detect my dishonesty. I was never any good at lying.

"Hi, I'm Ms. Watkins. I'd like to speak to someone about enrolling my younger sister for the fall semester." I had initially planned to use a fake name but decided against it in case he asked for ID.

"I need to see some ID," he asked.

My inner self gave me the thumbs up for quick thinking. I pulled out my driver's license and showed it to him. Thank God I had gotten a New York State driver's license, even though I didn't have a car.

He took a quick look at my ID and gave it back to me. He pointed to an office down the hall and told me to go there to inquire about registration. It was a long hallway, and the sound of my heels clicking against the hard floor that had been buffed to a high gloss shine seemed deafening. As I fought off ancient memories of when I cheered at football games in front of my parents, I stopped to look at some pictures of students in a science lab in a glass showcase on the wall. A man in the picture caught my eye—I presumed he was the teacher. As I studied the picture more closely, I felt dizziness rise up in me, and I almost fainted. It was Andre's face in the picture. I couldn't believe it. I glanced at the date stamp on the photograph—it was from April. The picture had been taken only a few months ago.

My cell phone vibrated against my side through my purse. I reached in and dug it out. Janice was calling.

"Hi, Janice."

"You're never going to believe this!" she shouted. "They both attended Park East High School. Did you get there yet?"

"Yes, and you won't believe what I found, either, but I can't discuss it right now," I said looking around to be sure no one was within earshot.

"You can't give me a little hint?" she pleaded.

"No. I'm sorry, but I can't."

"Okay, be careful," she warned.

"I will ... and Janice?"

"Yes?"

"Thanks a bunch. I owe you one."

I ended the call and stuffed the phone back down into my purse. I stared back at that picture of the man who looked exactly like Andre. They really could have been twins. That anonymous caller hadn't lied about that. Who *was* the anonymous caller? Could he be someone who worked at the school? No wonder Charlie was so insistent that Andre left the murder scene. I don't see any differences between the two. Same hair, same smile. Oh my God! Could this teacher be the real killer? Who is he? My mind was spinning with questions.

A student walked down the hall toward me. He was tall and thin with a bad case of acne, and he had a gap between his two front teeth when he smiled.

"Hi," I said.

"Hi," he said pleasantly.

I pointed to the man in the picture. "Do you know him?" I searched his face for a response.

"I never had him for class, but I know who he is. That's Mr. Peterson. He teaches biology."

"Is he here today?" I needed to see this person up close and in person.

"It's your lucky day." The boy laughed. "Yep, he's here. I just passed by his class a few minutes ago."

"Where can I find him?" I asked.

He pointed. "Go down that hall over there and up the stairs. He's in room two-oh-three."

"Thank you so much, young man. You've been a great help." I offered a smile.

He smiled back and continued walking down the hall in the opposite direction.

I took out my cell phone, lined up the shot, and captured Mr. Peterson on my phone. "Gotcha," I whispered.

I then took the stairs two at a time up to the second floor. The hallway was empty. I walked down the hall, searching for the room. I was two doors away, and my heart felt as if it was going to burst from my chest. I wasn't sure what I would do when I laid eyes on this Mr. Peterson, who looked strikingly like Andre.

As I got closer to the doorway of the biology room, I felt nervous. What if he saw me? What should I say to him? What if he recognized me as the journalist who wrote the story on the murders? I was being silly. Of course, he wouldn't recognize my face.

Oh my God! If he did rape and kill those girls, he was letting an innocent man go to jail for something that he did.

I walked closer and could see a few students sitting at their desks. I let my eyes roam the classroom, and I saw him standing by the window ledge, facing the class. He spoke, answering a question from one of the students. Not only was his voice similar to Andre's, his mannerisms were identical—he was a dead ringer for Andre. He wore black pants and a short sleeved pale blue shirt.

I caught my breath and leaned against the wall to keep from passing out. I heard him call out.

"Hey, are you all right out there?"

I pulled myself together and ran down the hallway and back down the stairs. I quickly exited the school building and sat outside on the steps to calm down and try to soak it all in. I felt as if I were in a nightmare that kept getting eerier. I grimaced at the pain in my head. My mouth was bone dry. I reached in my purse for the bottle of water I had been lugging around and took a few sips. My cell phone vibrated as I swallowed the last drop. I couldn't remember ever receiving so many phone calls in one day. I didn't quite recognize the number, but I pushed the button to answer the call anyway.

"Hello?"

"Nicole?"

The voice sounds familiar, but who is it? "Yes, this is Nicole," I answered as I tried to remember where I had heard the voice before.

"Hi. This is Robert, Andre's father. I received your messages and talked with Andre. Sorry I took so long getting back to you. It's been an extremely difficult day."

"Hello, Mr. Moore. Thanks so much for returning my call. Andre said you were going to tell me where and what time he will be arraigned today."

203

I tried to keep my voice steady. I wasn't sure whether to reveal to him over the phone what I had just witnessed or wait until I saw him personally. I decided to wait and tell him everything when I saw him, including what Charlie had told me.

"Well, I'm headed over to the courthouse now to meet up with his attorney. You can meet us there."

He gave me the address where I should meet up with them. Since I had plenty of time to get there, I decided to take a walk down to the subway station and take the train there. It would give me time to calm down and gather my thoughts.

I looked back at the high school and shivered.

I needed to act fast before Mr. Peterson selected his next victim.

CHAPTER 19

The courthouse on Centre Street in Manhattan was a massive building that stood seventeen stories high. As luck would have it, Robert Moore was standing outside of the courthouse talking with another man dressed in an expensive designer suit much like Robert's. Both were older, attractive gentlemen. When I approached the two men, Robert Moore bent to give me a kiss on the cheek.

"Hello, Nicole. It's so nice to see you again." His smile was inviting.

"Hello, gentlemen," I said as I looked from one to the other.

"George, this is my son's girlfriend, Nicole Watkins. She's a journalist with *News Today*." He gestured toward the other man. "Nicole, this is my friend, George Caldwell, the attorney who will be handling Andre's case."

"Nice to meet you, Ms. Watkins," George replied as he extended his hand for me to shake.

"Same here. Please call me Nicole." My hand met his, and we shook.

"Um, I have some information that may help Andre's case," I blurted.

My comment was not directed toward either one of them in particular. At that exact moment, Robert Moore's cell phone rang, and he excused himself to answer it. There was an awkward silence between George and me while we waited for Robert to return to the conversation after he ended the call.

"I'm sorry, that was my wife, Monica. I had asked her to meet me here, and it appears that she's already inside the courthouse searching for me." He turned to face me. "Nicole, if it's all right with you, why don't you go ahead and fill George in on your findings while I go inside to find Monica. I'll meet you both inside."

"No, I don't mind at all."

I felt strangely relieved that I didn't have to witness the look on Mr. Moore's face when I started telling him about all the crazy things I had learned in the last twenty-four hours that could dramatically affect this case. I didn't want him to think I was some sort of lunatic who was making things up. I didn't care what the lawyer thought, as long as it was convincing enough to change things around for Andre.

"So, Ms. Watkins, um ... I mean, Nicole, what is it that you have to share?" the attorney asked.

I told him what Charlie told me about the tattoo, the anonymous phone call, and my trip to Park East—and Mr. Peterson.

Mr. Caldwell's eyes widened and the corners of his mouth curled upward into a small smile. "This is amazing! Are you absolutely sure, Nicole?" He beamed with joy.

"Yes, I'm absolutely sure." I showed him the picture on my phone.

"It certainly looks like Andre," Mr. Caldwell said.

Mr. Peterson said. "He's teaching a summer class, so he'll be easy to find."

Mr. Caldwell laughed. "I need to get this information ADA Grimes pronto. I also need to call my assistant to have him research a few things. You've already saved us some of the leg work."

He pulled me close, gave me a friendly hug, and patted me on the back. "Thank you, Nicole. Well done."

"Oh, there's one more thing," I said.

"Yes, what is it?"

"I had a coworker do a bit of research on the two girls who were murdered, and she discovered that they both attended Park East High School. I'd

207

be willing to bet that they both had Mr. Peterson as their teacher."

"Are you sure you don't want a job in law? Excellent job!" He smiled and walked into the building.

"No, thanks," I called after him.

I took my phone out and made a call to Blackman. This time, his secretary answered the phone and put my call straight through to him.

"I talked to Janice, and she told me you went to Park East. Where are you now?"

"The courthouse on Centre Street attending Detective Moore's arraignment."

"Why?" he growled. "The arraignment is only a formality. Get your behind back here, Watkins."

Geez, I'm about to give this man tomorrow's headline, and this is how he treats me? "I needed to meet with the detective's father and his attorney. I had news that might possibly clear Detective Moore of murder charges."

"What do you have?"

I repeated what I told Mr. Caldwell.

"Well, come in and write it now."

"But I might have a happy ending for my story", Mr. Blackman," I said. "How often does a journalist get that? Let me stay."

Mr. Blackman sighed. "I'll hold the front page for you. Good job, Watkins."

Click.

I entered the courthouse to freshen up in a crowded ladies' room. After peeing, I tidied up some oily spots on my face, reapplied my lipstick, and brushed my hair while women rushed in and out behind me. After washing my hands, I turned to leave as Monica burst into the bathroom, a phone glued to her ear.

"Yes, I *do* feel guilty about it," she was saying. She focused on me. "Um, I gotta go." She ended the call and dropped her phone into her purse. "Hi, um, Nicole, right?"

I nodded. I also balled up my fists. I wanted to hurt this woman for what she did to Andre.

"You're here to support Andre? That's so sweet of you." Monica fluffed her hair and squinted into a mirror.

"Yes." I went to the exit door and leaned against it. "That's me. Sweet and innocent." I stared at a run in her stockings. "Unlike you."

Monica turned to face me. "What's that supposed to mean?"

"I know what you did to Andre," I said.

Monica blinked rapidly. "You do?"

"Yes."

"And what did I *do* to Andre?"

"You drugged and seduced him seven years ago."

Monica sighed. "Is that what he told you?" She shook her head. "You *are* sweet and innocent. And naïve. Andre and I got drunk *together*, and we made a mistake *together*. I didn't drug him." She posed. "Look at me. I don't need to drug anyone."

Doubt crept through my veins. "I don't believe you."

"Andre had the biggest crush on me," Monica said.

"Wasn't it the other way around?"

Monica's eyes darted to the ceiling and back. "Hey, we're going to be late. I'm here to support my husband in his time of need."

"You forgot all about him that night with Andre," I said.

"Okay, I didn't love Robert like I love him now." She widened her eyes. "Satisfied?"

"And what about Katie?"

Monica seemed to shiver. "What about her?"

I watched Monica's eyes flitting around the room as if they were trying to escape. "She's Andre's daughter, isn't she?"

Monica marched toward me. "This isn't the time or the place. The arraignment's about to start."

I stood my ground. "So it's true."

Monica's shoulders sagged.

Wow. It was *true!* "Andre thinks Katie is his stepsister."

"And he can never know otherwise," Monica pleaded. "Please. I'm not proud of what we did, and Robert can never know that he's not Katie's father."

"The truth will come out," I said.

"But not today, okay?" She moved closer to me. "Not when Katie's daddy is on trial for his life," she whispered. "Please let me out."

"Who were you talking to when you came in, Monica?"

"Nobody." She reached for the door handle.

"Somebody else knows, right?"

Monica nodded. "Yes."

"Someone you told?"

Monica threw her head back. "What does it matter now?" she moaned. "Let me out of here."

"Or what?"

Monica's chin dropped to her chest. "Please, Nicole. Let me by."

I stepped aside, and Monica ran out of the bathroom. She seemed to be in her feelings about this. I didn't believe that she told *anybody* about this on her own. Someone must have found out about it. *That's it.* That heifer is being blackmailed.

We reap what we sow.

****

When I entered the courtroom, everyone was already seated, and every seat was filled, reporters like me crammed into every possible seat. The wood paneled room buzzed with the conversations of reporters from Fox News, *the Daily News*, CNN, the *New York Times*, and assorted bloggers. Some seemed to be adjusting their equipment, while others engaged in conversation.

Monica sat next to Robert, her arm locked in his. It took everything in me not to go over there and expose her for the lying, cheating heifer that she was. How could she do a thing like that to both Andre and his father? Their lives would never be the same once they learned her secret. It was bad enough that she had drugged her own husband's son and slept with him, but to give birth to his child and pass the child off as his sister? She ought to rot in hell for that. I walked down the aisle and took a seat behind them.

Robert turned around to face me. He extended his hand. "Nicole, George told me that you gave him some information that may be very useful in my son's case. He hasn't had a chance to go into great detail about it, but he did speak with the assistant district attorney, and it looks very promising for Andre. I don't know how to thank you."

Monica turned to give me a snobby glare and a fake smile.

I smiled at Robert and gave Monica a blank stare.

The court proceedings had begun, and there were two or three cases called before Andre's. After a court officer led him into the courtroom, Andre glanced around the courtroom as he entered and our eyes met and locked. My heart skipped a beat as he gazed at me. How could a person have gone through so much hell in two days and still look so damn handsome? I'm glad he wasn't in his prison jumper but in a nice navy blue suit.

Andre's case was called, and he was charged with rape and murder in the first degree. I found myself holding my breath, and it seemed I wasn't the only one in the courtroom doing that. I have never heard a quieter courtroom.

"How does the defendant plead?" the judge asked.

Mr. Caldwell straightened his tie. "My client pleads—"

"Your honor, may I approach?" ADA Grimes interrupted.

The judge waved him forward.

Grimes spoke in a low voice to the judge. I

imagined he was giving her the information I had given Mr. Caldwell. The judge nodded her head, and Grimes stepped back.

"Go ahead, Mr. Caldwell," the judge said.

"The state is not charging Andre Moore at this time," Grimes said.

Reporters shouted, "Why?" The judge rapped her gravel, and Andre hugged Mr. Caldwell. Some reporters raced out the courtroom. I was so confused!

"What's going on?" I asked Robert.

"Andre can come home!" Robert stood and shouted, "Yes!" He then leaned forward and gave George and Andre big bear hugs.

My eyes filled with tears. *Thank you, God!* I was overjoyed, but I was still confused! They weren't charging him "at this time." What exactly did that mean? Could he still be charged in the future?

A few moments later, outside of the courtroom, we all gathered as we waited for Andre. He appeared shortly thereafter, that familiar smile of his glued to his face. He scooped me up in his arms and held me tight.

"Nicole. Thank you so much, baby, for all your help." He covered my lips with his and kissed me passionately in front of our audience.

I was flushed with embarrassment but welcomed

his kiss. Whatever issues we had that day on the plane before his arrest seemed of no importance now.

Andre was free!

****

Forllini's was crowed as usual, but it wasn't far from the courthouse. It was a great place to celebrate Andre's freedom. Italian spices permeated the air when we all entered. We didn't have to wait long to be seated in one of the red cushioned booths. Paintings of Italy and Italian people lined the wood paneled walls. I sat quietly next to Andre and squeezed his hand every chance I got while he, George, and Robert conversed. Monica sat next to Robert with a smug look on her face. I was happy to have Andre next to me. Our server took our orders of sautéed eggplant, stuffed mushrooms, artichoke hearts, mussels, pesto gnocchi tortellini alfredo, chicken scallopini marsala, and veal scallopini picatta.

"Why don't we all come back to my house after leaving here?" Robert asked. "We can have dessert there."

"I'm already full," I said. "Don't think that I could eat another bite."

"Andre, I know you can still put away more,"

Robert said. "We can order the dessert to go. Come on ... what do you say?"

"We're going to go all the way to Long Island for dessert when we can eat it here?" Andre asked.

I nudged Andre under the table with my leg because it seemed that Robert wanted to spend a little more time with him.

****

Robert switched on the big screen wall mounted TV when we entered the great room in the mansion. NBC was broadcasting a breaking news story.

We watched two uniformed officers escorting a man in handcuffs into the courthouse. When they demanded the camera's move back, we were able to see the man's face. It was Mr. Peterson, Andre's lookalike.

"What the hell?" Andre's face paled. "Who the hell was that?"

Robert became ill and slouched down onto a couch.

Monica gasped and screamed out, "Oh, my Lord!!"

When the officers paraded Mr. Peterson past the cameras, Andre stared transfixed at the screen. It seemed like a moment from the *Twilight Zone*.

Everyone in the room was in total shock except for me.

"What the hell did I just see?" Andre shouted.

"That was a teacher at Park East High School by the name of Mr. Peterson," I explained. "I think he's who Charlie saw that day."

"That's *not* what I'm talking about," Andre said. "Can someone *please* explain to me how it is that there is another person in this world who not only resembles me but is a carbon copy of me?"

Robert mumbled, "Not in a million years. I can't believe it. Oh my God!"

"Dad, are you okay?" Andre wiped away the sweat that had beaded on his forehead and knelt beside his father.

Robert straightened his posture and looked at Andre, tears in his eyes. "Son, there's something I need to tell you. Let's, um, let's go for a walk, and I'll—"

"Tell me now, Dad," Andre interrupted. "I want to know now." He touched his father's shoulder.

Robert began to shake. "Andre, when your mother got pregnant, we were both very young and poor. We could barely feed ourselves. When she went into labor and was taken to the hospital, the doctors found out she had been carrying two babies, not one."

"I have a twin?" Andre shouted.

Robert nodded. "Yes. Your mother never had a sonogram during the pregnancy, and the general practitioner who cared for her during her pregnancy didn't pick up the heartbeats of two babies. So all along, we thought she was pregnant with only one child." He took a handkerchief from his pocket and blew into it.

Andre appeared stunned. He stood. "And the man on the TV—he's my twin?"

"He might be, I don't know," Robert said.

"Might be?" Andre pointed at the TV. "I was looking into a mirror just now."

Robert dropped his chin to his chest. "Son, please," Robert begged. "It was the hardest decision that your mother and I ever had to make. We were very poor and couldn't afford a family, but your mother begged and pleaded that we keep at least one of our babies. We put our other son up for adoption. We wanted both of you, son. You have to believe that." His eyes filled with tears. "Your mother suffered so much with the decision that we made." He stood and attempted to rest his hand on Andre's arm, but Andre snatched it away.

"Who makes a decision to separate twin babies and raise only one? Who does that, Dad? Who?" Tears flowed from Andre's eyes.

"Andre—"

"Don't you say another word to me!" Andre interrupted. "I can't hear any more. I hate you for what you did!" Andre stormed through the living room, burst through the double doors, and went outside.

I caught up with him outside. He was so distraught. His world would never be the same again, and this was only the beginning.

"Andre?" I touched his hand.

He pulled me close to him, hugged me tightly, and wept.

I held him and let him cry.

"I'm so sorry, baby. I'm so sorry," I murmured. "We're going to get through this together. You're going to be fine."

I wished I believed that.

******

Three weeks passed since Andre found out he had a killer twin brother. During those weeks, I thought about telling him Katie was his daughter, but I couldn't bring myself to do it. I don't know if he could have taken another blow to the heart so soon. I would let him know when the time was right, when I thought he was strong enough to handle it.

I had just walked out of Blackman's office after receiving a pay raise when my cell phone rang. It was

Andre, and he wanted me to meet him for lunch. He suggested we meet up at Sassy's, the bar and grill where I had introduced him to Janice and Joann.

When I arrived, he was already there, sitting at the bar and sipping what appeared to be an iced tea. I walked over to him and kissed him softly on his lips.

"Hello, handsome." I winked at him.

"Hello, beautiful." He placed one hand on my butt and squeezed gently.

"What is that you're drinking?" I asked.

"Iced tea." He grinned.

"You're sitting at a bar drinking iced tea?" I laughed.

"Yep. I'm still on the job." He kissed me again. "I think they have a table ready for us now."

After being seated, we talked for a little bit before Andre slipped a black velvet box from his pocket.

My heart leaped from my chest.

He walked to my side of the table and got on one knee as the people around us stared and smiled at us. He opened the box to show a beautiful diamond ring that sparkled brilliantly in the light.

He took one of my hands in his. "Nicole, will you marry me?" he asked with a bright smile.

I wanted to shout "Yes!" at the top of my lungs, but I couldn't because I knew something he needed to know first. How could I marry him without him knowing my secret? He didn't know about Katie, and I didn't want to hurt him all over again.

I had no idea what to do.

Then my inner self shouted at me, *You're not marrying him today, fool! You'll have plenty of time to explain it to him before you get married! Now take the damn ring!*

I felt a teardrop of joy roll down my cheek. I had never been so happy or so much in love.

"Yes," I said softly, and the tears began to flow.

Andre took the ring from the box and placed it on my finger. "Thank you for saying yes."

I held his face gently in both of my hands and kissed him passionately as the people in the background cheered and clapped their hands.

"Well," I said breathlessly, "you really gave me no other choice ..."

The End

Dear Reader,

I hope you enjoyed MIRRORED. As an author, I love feedback. So tell me what you liked, what you loved, even what you hated. I'd love to hear from you. You can write me at daliafloreabooks@gmail.com and visit me on the web at daliafloreabooks.com.

I need to ask a favor. If you're so inclined, I'd love a review of MIRRORED. Loved it, hated it. I'd just enjoy your feedback.

Reviews can be tough to come by these days. You, the reader, have the power now to make or break a book.

Thank you so much for reading MIRRORED and for spending time with me.

In Gratitude,
Dalia Florea

Other books by Dalia Florea

Teardrops Know My Name
Whatever Dude
Reflections – Coming 2017

ABOUT THE
AUTHOR

Dalia grew up in Queens, New York and now makes her home in Northern Virginia outside of Washington, D.C. She is the author of Mirrored,

Teardrops Know My Name and Whatever Dude! Her debut, Mirrored reached Amazon's Bestseller's list in Women's Detective Fiction. Her second novel, Teardrops Know My Name also reached Amazon's Bestseller's list in African American Mystery, Thriller and Suspense. Her third book, Whatever Dude! a short fun read about her online dating experience was also an Amazon Bestseller. She is an avid reader who enjoys writing fiction stories with a mixture of mystery and suspense sprinkled with romance. When she isn't crafting mystery suspense stories with a dash of romance, she enjoys reading, attending live music concerts, visiting wineries and solving puzzles.

Visit her at www.daliafloreabooks.com
Facebook: https://www.facebook.com/pages/
Dalia-Florea-Author/411778885621667?ref=hl
Twitter: @DaliaFlorea
Instagram: DaliaFlorea
Pinterest: Dalia Florea

A CHAPTER FROM TEARDROPS KNOW MY NAME

Chapter 1

Linda McNair shrieked, bounced from her chair, and did a happy dance around her desk. She'd gotten the job. She'd gotten the job every freelance fashion photographer in New York City had wanted.

She claimed her seat again, but only because she had to make sure her eyes weren't deceiving her. She'd been feeling duped all day by the insistent barrage of anonymous text messages she'd been receiving. Anxiety about those messages threatened to creep in, but she shrugged it off. She had good news. Good news she'd been waiting for. She reread the message:

Linda,

Your portfolio and references were both impressive. Ross Brothers decided to go with your studio for the fall print shoot. I'm jumping on a plane, but let's plan to talk first thing Monday morning about the particulars. We're on a tight deadline to get the catalog done, so lace up your roller skates. Have a great weekend and congrats!

Bo

She let her head drop back and whispered a silent prayer. It wasn't even the end of the January, and her New Year's plan to double her freelance income was already coming to fruition. All she'd had to do was put the word out that she was looking for work, and it was practically falling in her lap. She could hardly believe it.

Linda folded her arms over her chest and leaned back against the cool leather headrest on her chair. Who would have thought shy, introverted, Linda McNair, who grew up in Seattle sheltered by her parents would have this much career success at her age. Twenty-nine was young in any field, but in the world of fashion photography, most artists her age were still looking for their first assistant job with an established photographer. But not her. She'd taken a chance on doing her own thing for a few years after college, then had signed on with *Flaunt Magazine*, and her portfolio had grown and grown.

Her phone beeped to announce a new text message, and she froze. Her heart began to pound in rapid beats, and her arms tensed up. All the joy she'd just been feeling evaporated from her soul. *Not again*, she thought.

Linda was beginning to hate her cell phone and her office phone. Phones were becoming the enemy, but she couldn't ignore them. They were a necessity. She bit her lip and reached for her cell. Relief flooded her when she saw it was a message from her boyfriend, Steve. *Thinking about the day I met you. Best day of my life and it's been the best two years of my life.* An anniversary. This was a first. She'd never been involved with a man for this long in her entire life. But Steve was special. She'd recognized that the first day she met him.

She had stopped in for lunch that afternoon at her favorite carryout restaurant and was flying from the counter to the door in a rush to get back to her studio when she'd run right into another customer.

"Oh my God!" Linda shrieked. She couldn't believe she'd been such a klutz. She looked down at the mess her spilled ice tea had made all over the floor and then let her eyes follow the upward trail to the soaked slacks of the man in front of her. She was horrified. But as her eyes continued their upward path to meet his, the adrenaline shot through her veins. It wasn't just because the man she'd nearly assaulted was so tall and good-looking, or because his skin was sun-kissed and flawlessly tanned like he'd just returned from a vacation to Bora Bora. Nor was it the way his athletic body had felt pressed against hers when she'd slammed against it, or how perfectly his dirty blond hair lay. No. Those attributes, though stunning, weren't the ones that had mesmerized her. It was those piercing, cool blue eyes that had nearly hypnotized her on the spot, and even though their color wasn't warm, they emitted a gentle heat that said he'd forgiven her even before she'd asked. Linda felt winded but managed to speak her pitiful apology. "I am so sorry."

Their gazes locked for a moment, but when released, she noted his quick once-over of her from head to toe before he smiled and putting his amazingly white teeth on display. *More perfection*, she had thought. Everything about him said 'pulled together'—except, now, for his suit. Thanks to her. She reached into her handbag for her wallet. "Please let me pay for your dry cleaning." She removed a twenty dollar bill.

He raised a hand to hers, curling her fingers around the twenty, and said, "That won't be necessary."

Linda's breath caught at his touch. She dropped her eyes to his fingers, noting that he hadn't let her hand go. Magnetic. That's what this connection was. It scared her. She removed her hand. "I insist," she continued.

One of the restaurant's waitstaff came over with a mop. He looked annoyed that she'd made such a mess, so Linda apologized to him also.

She felt a hand on her elbow. The man she'd soaked from the knees down was pulling her out of the busboy's way. He leaned close to her ear and said, "I'm Steve Mitchell, and you are?"

Linda followed him away from the mess, gently easing her elbow from his grasp. "I'm someone who feels awful for ruining your suit." She held the twenty dollar bill out again and said, "I'll feel horrible if you don't let me compensate you. It's only lunchtime. You'll be terribly uncomfortable all afternoon."

He leaned in again, and this time she caught a whiff of his cologne. A sexy, woodsy scent that she thought might be the new Giorgio Armani fragrance. "I keep a change in the office," he whispered. "A man has to be prepared for pretty women rushing about in this city."

Linda self-consciously licked her lips. "Well, I'm glad you won't be all sticky."

"Sticky, huh?" He flashed those white teeth at her again. "Not today." His voice was flirtatious. "I tell you what. You do owe me, so I was thinking there's something else you can do instead."

Linda cocked her head. He was talking of stickiness and something else she could do for him. She sure hoped his mind had not gone where she thought it had. "Look, I don't know what you have in mind—"

"Lunch," he said, cutting her off. "I had lunch in mind."

Linda's brow knit. He'd surprised her. "I didn't make enough of a mess of your wardrobe? Or do you ask every woman that you bump into to have lunch with you?"

Steve Mitchell chuckled. "Only the ones who take my breath away."

Linda pursed her lips. "Breathless often?" she asked.

Steve shook his head and replied, "Rarely."

She wasn't sure why she'd given him her business card that day. She had thought it was his obscenely good looks, but thinking back now, she realized it was the intensity with which he had released that single word from his lips. *Rarely.* In an instant, she'd felt unique and special. He'd seduced her in less time than it'd taken for that Styrofoam cup to hit the floor, and now, two years later, he was still doing it. He was still taking her breath away.

Linda smiled and sent a text back to him.

Happy Anniversary to you too.

Seconds after she sent it, another message came through. She smiled, thinking how thoughtful he was being today. But then, once she opened it, she swore under her breath. It was Marc, letting her know that he was at the restaurant where they were meeting for dinner.

She hated being late—especially for something with Marc. He was always reminding her that she was the definition of a stereotype. "Losers are on C.P. time," he'd say. And to make her lack of timeliness worse, this was a special night for him. They were celebrating his promotion. She cursed again and pressed a speed dial number. When he answered the call, there was so much noise in the background that she couldn't quite hear him clearly.

"Marc, if you can hear me, I'm running late. See you in a few." She hoped that he heard her.

She pushed her chair back, grabbed her nearby handbag, and rushed toward the door, pulling her jacket from the coat rack as she passed it. Before leaving, she turned and looked at the prints that were scattered across the conference room table. She was behind on her deadline to get the photos from the exclusive shoot with Victoria's Lingerie completed early, which meant she'd have to come back after dinner. There was no point in taking the time to shut down the computer. She pulled the door closed behind her and turned the key in the deadbolt.

The spot where they were meeting was within walking distance from her studio. The January wind whirled around, nipping at her face as she exited the building. She tightened her coat around her in an attempt to keep warm, but it wasn't working. She was shivering, and it wasn't just the cold. The street was unusually deserted for a Tuesday evening. Darkness had stolen the sun's rays away, and the dying streetlamp on the corner in front of her made a crackling sound that added to the eeriness.

Linda thought about the text messages and phone calls she'd received. She stopped in her tracks when she thought she heard a noise behind her. Heart slamming in her chest, she turned. No one there. She swallowed and made quick steps down the street to the restaurant. Just as she approached the door, her phone chirped in a text message. She reached into her pocket, thinking it was Marc, and removed her cell to check it.

A sad smiley face.

A violent shiver passed through her entire body. She swallowed. Instinctively, she looked around her and over her shoulder. Was someone following her? She dropped her phone into her bag and closed her eyes for a moment. *This is too much,* she thought. This has been going on for too long to be kids playing as she had originally suspected.

She pulled on the door to the restaurant and stepped inside. Instantly, the lobby's warmth and safety enveloped her. There were people here. Not as many as there usually were, but she spotted the one who would make her feel the safest. Marc was in the far right corner of the restaurant—one hand on a beer and the other on a newspaper, no doubt his favorite, the *Wall Street Journal.*

Linda released a cleansing breath, handed her coat to the coat check attendant, and made her way to the table.

Marc stood, as he always did when she approached the table, and she leaned in and kissed him on his cheek.

"Don't say it," she said.

"I got your call," Marc replied, pulling her chair

out. "You're going to be late to your own Photography Masters Cup event."

"Ha, ha," Linda said taking her seat. "I won't be late for that."

"You know we are whatever we do."

"Excellence then is a habit," Linda said, finishing the Aristotle quote he had begun. "I'm only late for personal stuff. I'm never late for business."

"Says you," Marc replied, folding his paper. He stared at her for a moment.

She became self-conscious, looking down at her cherry red dress to see if she'd spilled something on it. But she didn't see anything. "Is there something on my face?" she asked, touching the corners of her mouth.

"Nah, lil sis, you just look kind of pretty tonight."

Linda smirked. "Kind of?"

"Well, you know. As pretty as you can look to me." Marc raised his sweating glass and took a long sip of his beer. "Sometimes you come out of that studio looking like you been in a dark cave instead of a dark room."

Linda smirked again and picked up her menu. "All the better to serve our clients—" She stopped midsentence. "Clients! Oh my God . . . congrats on your deal!" She jumped up from her chair and reached over to give Marc a hug.

"I was starting to think you forgot."

Linda reclaimed her chair. Marc's lips spread wide, boasting a smile. "You're a rock star," she said. "I'm so proud of you."

Marc took another sip of his beer and said, "You know how we do it. Work hard, play later."

"I know, but even with working hard, landing *Ouch Magazine* was a big deal."

"Yeah, it was," Marc replied. "Maybe I can get you some work over there."

Linda picked up her menu and let out a long sigh. "That would be great, but sometimes I think I already have more than I can handle."

"You're too meticulous, girl. You need to push some of those photos out faster."

Linda let her shoulders drop. She and Marc had had this conversation before. He was a numbers man. There was no way he could understand that, as a photographer, her work took precision and time. She couldn't cut corners and rush through a program. She wasn't dealing with Excel or Access. She was creating art. "We've had this conversation before." She glanced at the menu and decided on the dish she always had before closing it. "It may be time for me to take on an intern."

"It's past time." Marc frowned. "I've been telling you that.

The waitress approached their table and, after some not so subtle flirting with Marc, took their orders. Marc was by far too good-looking a brother to be in the friend zone. He wasn't exceptionally tall, but he was tall enough for most women. He had great skin which made him look like a velvety smooth chocolate bar and dimples that would make any woman's heart flutter. Women friends were always surprised that he was so good-looking when she introduced him for the first time. They all quickly followed up with the question, "Are you guys dating or something?" Even though they knew about Steve.

"Nothing wrong with having vanilla *and* chocolate ice cream. They have a name for it—the swirl," one of her more brazen colleagues had stated. But Linda had never thought of Marc that way. She had already been involved with Steve when she met him, and Marc's initial approach was all business. He was a consultant, and she needed a new business plan. The fast friendship came as a result of them working together so closely.

Marc's phone rang, rousing her from her thoughts. He looked at it and said, "I have to take this, lil sis." Then he stood and walked away from the table.

Linda found that odd. He took business calls but rarely excused himself. She shrugged it off and pulled her own phone from her bag. She swiped the screen, and the sad smiley appeared again. It had been waiting for her like an omen that refused to go away. She closed the text message, closed her eyes, and dropped her head back. Fingers on her shoulder caused her to nearly jump out of her seat. She bumped the table so hard her water goblet spilled.

Marc hovered above her and then, after picking up her glass, said, "Damn, girl. You had that look like you needed somebody to work the kinks out of your neck."

Linda picked up a napkin and dabbed at the water puddle on the table. "I'm sorry."

"Why are you so jumpy?"

She shook her head. "I know this is going to sound crazy, but...someone is harassing me."

Marc raised an eyebrow. "What do you mean?"

"I mean, I'm getting weird phone calls and text messages. I feel like I'm being followed sometimes. I don't know. Something's going on."

Marc released a long plume of air, his brow knit in a frown. "How long has this been going on?"

"A while."

"A while . . . Like how long, Linda?"

She could see the concern etched on his face. She was grateful for it because it was more than she'd gotten from Steve. He'd dismissed the entire thing as kids playing on the phone and her overactive imagination. *You don't have an enemy on the earth, Linda. Who would follow you?* he'd said, and she'd cosigned to that for a while, but then the calls that had started on the office line began to come in on her cell phone. That wasn't kids. She shared her thoughts about it with Marc.

"So what about the police?" he asked, raising his beer again.

"What do I say? The number that comes up seems to be one of those scrambled numbers like the ones that those annoying telemarketers use, which leaves me with no real number to report. I haven't actually seen anyone following me. It's just a feeling."

Marc nodded.

"I have seen a strange car on my block lately. It drives by slowly and doesn't always park. It seems like it leaves when I come out the door or when I get home. It's weird."

Marc raised his eyebrows. "That part does sound like an overactive imagination. I mean, why would stalker leave when you show up? Don't they usually follow you?"

Linda shook her head. "I don't know how this works. I've never experienced it before. All I know is something is *not* right. I can feel it in my gut."

"Then you should report it." A beat of silence passed between them. "So what does Steve say about it?"

"He thinks I'm being paranoid," she replied, rolling her eyes.

"Is that so?" Marc said. "Typical."

"Don't start, Marc. I love him."

"The question is, does he love you?" Marc deadpanned, and she responded to his comment with the same intense stare.

"Of course he loves me. Why do you always have to question that?"

"Because you're scared as hell. Even I can see that, and your man isn't taking you seriously. That's why. I mean, I don't know about you being followed—a car in the neighborhood could be anything—but the phone calls on both phones is a bit much. Maybe it's a pissed off model or something." Marc finished his drink and picked up his phone. "I just got an email. I need to make a call." He stood again and left the table.

The food was delivered while he was gone. Linda

reached for the glass of wine the waitress had delivered for her and nearly downed it in one swig. Her hands shook, and she found herself looking at the door every time it opened. Marc was right. She was afraid.

He returned to the table, and her phone chirped a text. With her free hand, she reached into her bag for the cell. Linda dropped the wineglass when she read the message. Her vision blurred with the tears that instantly filled her eyes.

"Linda," Marc called. "What's wrong?"

She shoved the phone in his direction and watched as he studied it with a frown before reading it out loud. "Bitch, I hope you choke on a snail."

His eyes met her again. This time she saw more than a little concern. Seeing his fear made her entire body shake. "So, do you believe I'm being followed now?"

www.ingramcontent.com/pod-product-compliance
Lightning Source LLC
Chambersburg PA
CBHW030545200626
46808CB00024BA/264